Praise for Death's Too Short: Nine zombie Short Stories
By Lyle Perez-Tinics

I0519926

"Perez-Tinics gives us zombie tales that bring back the fun excitement of the genre. It's like being at the drive-in."
Mark Allan Gunnells, author of *Asylum*

"You would think the zombie premise is getting stale and overused wouldn't you? Well, you'd be wrong; Perez-Tinics does it different. This is a collection of stories with refreshing originality. At once gripping and harrowing, the stories don't rely on gore to grab the reader. The gore is provided of course, but as a compliment to the real brains of the stories. I want more!"
-Emma Ennis
http://www.AuthorEmmaEnnis.blogspot.com

The stories; *Vigor After Death*, *Fire Fighter*, *The Gingerbreads*, *Dead of Old*, and *Undead Side of the Moon* have been published in other anthologies, but the author holds all necessary rights to reprint.

ISBN 10 - 0615479863
ISBN 13 - 978-0-615479-866

Death ' s Too Short

Rainstorm Press http://www.RainstormPress.com
Copyright © 2011 by Lyle Perez-Tinics
All rights reserved.

Interior design by -
THE MAD FORMATTER
http://www.TheMadFormatter.com

Mini covers and cover concept done by Jessica Geis
Jgeis01@gmail.com

Mini covers for *Walker* and *Fire Fighter* are free stock images.

Cover art by Robert Elrod - http://www.RobertElrodLLC.com

Table of contents

Dr. Renbrick created a magical drug he named, Vigor. Vigor has the ability to heal any wound on the human body at an alarming rate. Now, he is on the hunt to test his drug on unsuspecting victims.

When the world dies and comes back to life, two brothers fight through hordes of living dead to find safety. Once they arrive at their safe haven, they turn to a local news broadcast that will change their lives forever.

Layne, a sixth grader, finds himself trapped inside his home with his father and stepmother while the dead walk the streets. A plan for escape is underway, but when trouble arises inside the home, the dead aren't the only threat to Layne.

The Zilith Corporation changed an asteroids' orbit to collide with the moon. The impact left behind enough raw materials to construct the Moonlit Resort. In 2059, Earth lost all communication with the moon-bound resort. Space Marshal Elroy Collins and his team are sent to investigate the disturbance.

It's Christmas and gingerbread cookies are alive, but so are the dead. Fred and Ginger witnessed a sight they thought they'd never see again ... human carolers. These 'normals' are hungry, but once they invade the home in search of cookies, the dead enter the home looking for human flesh.

Radio Dead

The Town of Bluebird County is being overrun by the recently dead coming back to life and seeking human flesh. The Manny Mayhem Morning Show is trapped in the radio station. There's no one left to save them, what do they do? Continue the show until they're all dead.

Dead of Old

It has been one year since the plague that brought the dead back to life was contained and the remaining dead were locked in a research facility. Life was starting to go back to normal until the infected escape. Joe, a former cameraman for the KBD News, must relive the nightmare that almost brought the human race to extinction.

Fire Fighter

Wildfires have been threatening Darrel's family ranch ever since he was a small child. Now that his parents are both death, it's up to him to work the farm alone. After being visited by a demon and a pack of dead firefighters, Darrel realizes that his father had other plans for their ranch after his demise.

Walker

Sergeant Val Walker and his Special Forces Team are sent into the heart of an infected town. Their mission is to learn about the infected and figure a way to bring them down. But after only an hour of arrival, his team is overrun. Now it's a fight for survival as Walker tries to save a lone survivor who is trapped on the roof of a pawnshop.

VIGOR AFTER
DEATH

Author Note:

Vigor After Death will always have a special place in my heart. It is the very first story I wrote from beginning to end. I originally wrote it for an inclusion in a May December Publications, LLC anthology. Ultimately, I decided not to sell this story to them. After that, *Vigor* sat on the shelf for a while until I submitted it to an anthology entitled, *Rhonny Reaper's Creature Features*. My story was accepted and published with Zilyon Press in 2011. I am happy with the response from this story and I'm proud to say this was my first foray into writing.

Vigor After Death

"Keep running!" Tony yelled across the field to Jeremy. "He's still behind us!" They maneuvered as best as possible in the dark. Their feet kicked dust into the air with every step they took.

The tall, hefty man had begun chasing them as they walked past a large cabin on the side of the trail.

"There!" Tony pointed to his right, looking back to Jeremy, who had started to catch up. "Run toward the woods!"

As they made their way into the small patch of wooded area, their moonlit vista darkened. The only light now came from the pale moonlight that shone through the leafy cover of the woods. A white mist materialized at their feet. Jeremy couldn't see the tree stump entombed in the ground before him. He tripped and fell face first to the dry earth, snapping his head back as he landed. Tony heard him fall and doubled back to help.

"I ... I can't keep running. I'm so tired. I need to rest," Jeremy said as Tony lifted him to his feet.

They both looked behind them; the man was nowhere in sight. They faced each other with a shared sigh of relief.

"All right, let's stay here for a bit." Tony pointed to a large oak tree to his right. "Lean up against that tree and dust

7

yourself off."

Jeremy followed Tony to the tree and leaned his back against the bark. He hunched over and took deep, agonizing breaths.

Tony placed a hand on his friend's shoulder. "Stay here. I'll go make sure that guy's really gone."

Jeremy gave him a sign of approval, and then continued to face the ground. Only when Tony walked around the tree did he realize how short a distance they'd ran. The large cabin they'd passed earlier was still visible. Through the darkness and fog, he could see the cabin's silhouette amongst the trees.

Tony turned back around to face Jeremy. "I don't see him anymore, I think we los—"

Before he could finish his sentence, he made out the man emerging from the growing mist. Chills ran up and down their backs as the man approached. The seven-foot-tall Leather Face look-alike smiled as he waved his knife back and forth.

Tony took a few steps back while his friend remained hunched over trying to re-gain his breath. Jeremy gathered enough strength to slam his shoulder into the stranger. Neither Tony nor their attacker expected that. Jeremy put enough force in-to the shove that it knocked the man off balance. The knife, which was nearly as big as Tony's size twelve shoes, fell to the ground. Jeremy ran hastily to Tony's side.

Jeremy's assault confused the man, but

after a moment he collected himself and continued to look at them angrily. They stared at each other, neither wanting to make the first move.

"Do we run?" Jeremy asked.

"No, this guy's just going to keep chasing us. We're going to have to knock him out, or kill him ..." his voice trailed off.

"Kill?"

The man scanned the ground, searching for the knife. The darkness and mist proved impenetrable, so he knelt and felt the ground with his hands. After a few moments of searching, the man stood. Another smile crossed his face as he revealed two empty hands, which he quickly clenched into fists.

"Now's as good a time as any," Jeremy said, cracking his knuckles.

Without warning, Tony rushed into the man. He was the smallest of the three, no taller than five foot six and with a slight frame. The sight of him trying to bring the behemoth down would have been comical had the men not been in such danger. But with the adrenaline pumping through his veins and fear in his eyes, Tony was determined to overpower the stranger.

Jeremy watched the two wrestle and braced himself for the fight, something he hadn't done in years. He had been forced into early retirement from mix martial arts fighting after fracturing his left leg in two different places. Strenuous exercise was a thing of the past for him, and it showed in the slight softness of his figure.

He jumped in just as the man escaped Tony's grip and overpowered him. The man forced Tony's head toward the ground, his grip unbroken even after Tony's body fell limp on the cold dirt.

Jeremy ran in swinging and landed a punch to the cheek that forced the man to stagger backwards. The pain in his knuckles gave him a quick flashback to his training, when he used to punch meat slabs hanging in his father's butcher shop. The pain evaporated, drowned in a cocktail of adrenaline and anger that jolted through his body.

As the man stumbled, Tony regained his feet. With one quick glance, they wordlessly agreed on a plan. They needed to find the knife and bring their attacker to the ground. Tony searched for the knife as Jeremy stood toe to toe with the man, prepared for a one-on-one fight.

The man's blank eyes stared right at Jeremy as if peering into his soul. He lunged forward, throwing wild punches. Jeremy did a good job dodging them until one of the man's blows found the side of his head. Enraged, Jeremy attacked. One after the other, Jeremy's jabs made contact with the man's face. They didn't seem to be doing much damage. It was as if the man's face were covered by a few extra layers of skin. Jeremy switched to uppercuts. The pain in his hands returned as his fists purpled.

"I can't find the fucking knife!" Tony yelled. Giving up the search, he turned in the direction of the fight. He had a good view of the man's back. The knife that he had been frantically searching for had been sheathed on the man's belt.

Horrified, Tony watched as the man reached for the knife. With one swift movement, the man slashed at Jeremy's left leg. Blood leaked from the slit in Jeremy's blue jeans. The weight of his upper body was more than his hacked leg could bear, and he collapsed to the ground. Jeremy's screams echoed within Tony's ears, but he could do nothing but stare as his friend was mutilated. The man slashed at Jeremy's right leg, immobilizing him.

Tony snapped out of his terrified stupor and lunged toward his friend, but the same stump that had tripped Jeremy earlier sent him sprawling. His head smashed into a large rock on the ground splitting his scalp open. Blood began pouring out of his wound and leaked onto the rock and ground around him. Tony's vision quickly darkened as he lay on the ground, motionless and in pain. His pain soon began to fade as he fell into an eternal sleep.

The man looked down at Jeremy and then looked around the woods. After a few seconds, the man concluded that Tony had run for his life.

Jeremy writhed on the ground, his body finally succumbing to the exhaustion and pain. The man sheathed his knife and knelt beside Jeremy.

"You'll do well," the man said with a slurred deep voice. "You'll do *very* well."

The man picked up the bloody mess that was Jeremy and flung him over his shoulder.

"Now it's time for you to meet my boss. Don't worry. You'll like him, and I'm sure you'll be the one. Yes ... you might very well be the one." The man's voice trailed off and ended with a horrid laugh. The man looked to his left then to his right. He walked down the path through the trees and at that very moment Jeremy fell unconscious.

* * *

Jeremy awoke with two men's voices ringing in his ears. He lay strapped down to a metal table, face up and immobilized. All he could see was a big bright white light.

"You brought only one?"

"Yes, sir. The other one got away from me. I got the better of the two, though. He's already damaged; let's see if your serum can cure his wounds."

"My serum has a name. Use it!"

"I'm sorry, sir."

"You should be. I should have left you where I found you, wandering the cold streets begging the townsfolk for scraps! This is not how I raised you, Neil."

"I understand, sir, please forgive me I implore you."

"You're like the son I never had, Neil

Please forgive me. You know I lose my temper when someone speaks ill of my life's work. *Vigor* will change the world. And I believe what I hold in my hand is the final product; with this last specimen you brought me, I will at last see Vigor in action. You and I, Neil, will be the first to witness this ..."

He paused and looked over to Jeremy.

"Ah look, our little friend's awake." He leaned in closer to look at his face. "Tell me, boy, what is your name?"

"My legs, I ... I can't feel them. Who are you? What do you want with me?"

"I'm doctor Renbrick, and you know what I want from you? Hmm, What I want is your goddamn name, deviant!" He wrapped his hands around Jeremy's neck and choked him.

"Jeremy, Jeremy ... My name is Jeremy!"

Renbrick let go. "Well, Jeremy, was that so hard? If you answer all my questions, there will be no more need for violence. Now where are you from, Jeremy?"

"I'm from Sea City." The answer came quickly.

"Oh just over the mountain there, not too far away. What were you and your friend doing in these parts of the woods? Don't you know there are dangerous people around here?" A smile crossed his face as he finished.

"I ... We were on a hike. We got lost and time flew by. We found the trail again, and we were on our way back home when this big Leather Face fucker started chasing us."

13

"Do you hear this, Neil? Leather Face ..." Renbrick snarled a deep laugh. "They called you Leather Face. Well I'll tell you this, Jeremy, Leather Face is a fictional character made up for the movies. Neil, on the other hand, is *all* too real. Poor guy had his face bitten off by vicious birds. But I fixed him up quite well; he was my first masterpiece. I used the flesh of corpses to patch him up. You'd be surprised how much power dead tissue has when combined with living cells. But that's not the point here."

"What is the point? What are you going to do to me? Why can't I feel my legs?" Tears ran down Jeremy's face.

"You, my friend, are the one who will change the world. You can't feel your legs because Neil did a number on you with his knife. Your legs are numb from the sedative I gave you. Don't worry, it will wear off at any moment, and then the fun begins." He reached into his coat pocket and withdrew the vial of Vigor. "This right here, will kill all the cells that are trying to heal your legs. You will feel tremendous pain as your condition worsens. Once the cells are dead, they will reanimate with the ability to heal your legs at an accelerated rate, almost instantaneously, in fact."

"What are you talking about?"

"Jeremy, less talking from you would be best right now, but I'll answer your question. I'm talking about taking your frayed, useless legs and healing them in a

flash. You'll feel pain at first while
your cells stop trying to heal, but after
that ... you'll recover. When the leg re-
generation proves successful, we will kill
you and see if Vigor has the power to
bring *you* back to life."

"That's crazy!" Jeremy snapped. "You're
going to kill me just to see if I'll come
back? What do you plan on accomplishing
with that?"

"LIFE!" Renbrick exclaimed. "I will be
able to bring the recently dead back to
life. Imagine your dead father, your girl-
friend, anyone to whom you've had to say
farewell coming back to life. People will
no longer be afraid of death."

Jeremy felt pain returning to his legs.
He grinded his teeth and writhed as he at-
tempted to move his head to locate his
captors. His vision diminished.

"Ah, I see you're starting to feel the
pain. I think it is time we begin."

Renbrick opened the vial and brought it
up to Jeremy's lips. "Now drink this like
a good boy, and in five minutes you'll be
back to normal, I promise."

Jeremy tried to keep his mouth closed,
but Neil joined Renbrick at Jeremy's side
and forced his jaw open. Drop by drop, the
Vigor slid down his throat. Once the vial
was empty, Neil and Renbrick stepped back
to watch the results. Jeremy's body shook
violently against the restraints. The
screams that ripped from his chest were
like nothing Renbrick or Neil has ever
heard. Finally, after five minutes of

screaming and shaking, Jeremy laid still, as if he were dead.

"That was quite a show wasn't it, Neil?"

"Yes it was, sir. Did it work?"

"I won't know for sure right away, but let's take a closer look at his legs."

Neil reached for the pair of scissors on the counter behind him. He cut the legs of Jeremy's pants so that the wounds were better exposed.

"Yes," Renbrick exclaimed, delighted. "They are almost completely healed. It's working. My God, IT'S WORKING!"

As he continued his examination, however, Renbrick's excitement faltered. "Wait a minute, no ... NO! This is all wrong. Neil, look at his legs; it's starting to get worse. This can't be. HOW CAN THIS BE?! He has no heartbeat, no ... no he can't be ..." Renbrick pounded on Jeremy's chest. "Breathe, goddammit, don't you stop the fight now!" Before long, Renbrick realized he had killed his specimen.

"He's gone ... I guess he wasn't the one after all."

"Sorry, sir," Neil said as he returned the scissors to the counter. "Something must have gone wrong."

"Yes, I know that, Neil," Renbrick spat. "Untie that piece of shit and make him a grave with the rest of the trash."

Renbrick murmured to himself, "Everything was right. What went wrong?"

Neil noticed something odd as he undid Jeremy's restraints.

"Sir, his face is twitching."

"What?" Renbrick glowed with excitement. "Let me see."

They hovered over Jeremy's body, waiting for him to move again. Jeremy's eyes opened. A white gloss gleamed over his irises. He seemed to be in a daze. His mouth flopped open revealing his dry tongue.

"Jeremy?" Renbrick said, leaning closer. "Can you hear me? Do you understand what's ...?"

Before Renbrick could finish, Jeremy lunged at him like a wild animal. Renbrick took a step back, but Jeremy caught hold of his arm and yanked Renbrick to him. Renbrick screamed as Jeremy sank his teeth into the arm and ripped off a piece of flesh. Jeremy's mouth chewed his prize and swallowed as Renbrick yanked back his arm.

"What the fuck is this? Neil, take care of this fucker while I bandage my arm."

"Yes, sir."

Neil grabbed his knife and walked up behind Jeremy. With his left arm, he put the captive in a head lock; with his right, he held the point of his knife to Jeremy's chest.

"Remember this?"

Neil stabbed repeatedly, and blood splattered around the room. Neil thrust the knife into Jeremy's chest a few more times before slicing him down to his stomach, revealing his rib cage and intestines. Neil pulled his knife from Jeremy's body and pushed him to the ground. His insides flopped on the tiled floor before Jeremy's body.

"It is done, sir. Do you want me to dispose of the body now, or do you want it for research?" There was no answer. "Sir, are you all right?"

Neil looked around the lab, but Renbrick was gone.

"Sir," he called out. "Where are you? It is done; what about the body?"

Neil walked into Renbrick's private office at the end of the lab. Renbrick, with his arm freshly bandaged, sat slumped in his chair, his body hunched over his desk as if he'd just laid down for a nap.

"Sir, I need orders. Shall I leave you to your nap?"

There was no answer. Neil walked closer to Renbrick, extending a hand to get the doctor's attention. Renbrick's chair slid back with a loud scrape and he stood, his eyes white with the same gloss that had shone in Jeremy's eyes. Neil took a step back and lifted his knife.

"Sir, are you going to attack me like Jeremy did you?"

A rumbling moan began in Renbrick's stomach and slowly surfaced out of his mouth.

"I don't know what's going on, sir, but I'm frightened. I'll leave you to your studies until you feel better. I'll go bury the body."

Renbrick walked slowly toward the retreating Neil. His eyes fixed on Neil as if he were food and Renbrick hadn't eaten

in days. Neil bolted for the door, but
stopped short when his eyes met the horror
of Jeremy's body walking toward him,
trailing viscera from the gaping wound
Neil had carved.

"What the hell? No, you're dead ... I
killed you!" Neil was trapped. Jeremy's
body was getting closer to the door, and
Renbrick was closing in from behind.

"Sir, please snap out of this insan-
ity."

Renbrick stretched out his arms and
grabbed Neil by the shoulders. Neil felt
as though his legs were glued to the
ground and chills rolled on his back when
he felt the doctor's touch. He couldn't
believe the horrors surrounding him in the
lab he called home. Neil's eyes closed,
and tears ran down his reconstructed face.
Renbrick leaned in and bit into Neil's
warm neck. Blood ran down his mouth as he
chewed, and a big piece of flesh came free
off Neil's neck. Neil's screams were si-
lenced when Jeremy bit into his throat,
tearing out his Adam's apple in one swift
movement. He fell to the floor, taking his
still-chewing assailants with him. Within
a matter of minutes, Neil died of blood
loss. Renbrick who sat on the cold floor
was still enjoying his meal when Neil's
eyes opened.

The three reanimated corpses wandered
through the lab until they found the way
out. By this time, morning had arrived.
The sun had risen over the horizon, but
dark clouds were moving in from the north.

The walking corpses did not acknowledge each other, even when they bumped into one another on their slow journey through the door. Only one impulse lived in their instinct-driven minds: their hunger, their need to feed on the flesh of the living.

A police siren erupted beyond the mountains. The sound caught their attention, and their instincts informed them that food could be found in that direction. The three walking dead that had once been Jeremy, Renbrick and Neil made their way toward the noise. A terrible fate awaited the citizens of Sea City as the corpses approached. They were the first infected; they brought Vigor after death.

Author Note:

Broadcast of the Dead was my second completed story. It was originally written to be a novel. *Vigor After Death* was the prologue for the story. Now that you've read *Vigor*, you know that Tony trips over a tree stump and dies. The original story was written so Tony was only knocked out. Later in the novel, Tony would hook up with the characters of *Broadcast of the Dead* to try to find a cure for Vigor, the drug that started everything. That never panned out and I decided to leave the stories separate. In the end, I do enjoy both endings.

Broadcast of the Dead

We've barricaded the front door with my living room furniture and then boarded up the windows. My brother, Stuart, and I locked ourselves in my upstairs master bedroom. I have no idea what's going on out in the streets, but I'm glad we made it to my house. What I witnessed today was the most horrifying experience of my life. Stu and I are sitting in the room waiting for the news broadcast to start. Maybe they'll be able to tell us what's going on or offer some good information. I still have time to kill so I'm leaning back on my bed and thinking about everything that has happened the past few hours.

* * *

I had just finished my usual ten-hour work shift at the Harrison Law Office building. I was not a lawyer nor a paralegal, but the building's maintenance man. A Janitor was the term I always preferred. Despite my criminal background, I was well accepted. But there were a few folks who didn't like the idea of an ex-con working next to them. Even if I did keep the toilets clean and made sure the floors were properly vacuumed.

I was no one special, but my boss, Mr. Harrison, really took a shine to me. Back in my criminal days, Mr. Harrison was my legal adviser. He did lose my case, but I never held it against him. I did the crime so I had to do the time. He did promise me work after my release though.

Mr. Harrison was nice enough to give me my very own parking space. The building's parking lot was in the basement, the spaces were reserved for attorneys only, so it was no surprise they were steamed when Mr. Harrison gave me a spot. The shutter doors in the parking lot open when a car needs to come in or out. If I was parked out in the streets, instead of in my parking spot, I would have been a dead man.

I glanced at my watch. It was precisely 7:00 P.M.

"Time to go home." There was no one in the office with me, so my words were only heard by me.

The Harrison Law Office's workday ended at five-o'clock, so every day I was alone to lock up the building. This time of year it's always dark when I head home. I never had a problem with the dark. It never scared me as a kid so I didn't mind being alone at the end of the day.

I finished double checking the windows and doors to make sure they were all secured. I walked toward the alarm keypad and began to set it. The beeping noise from the alarm arming blared out of the device. I walked, in unison with the beep, as I headed toward the exit. I made my way through the door, and turned to lock it.

24

The beeping was still heard through the door as I waited for it to arm. I always did this; I'm a very cautious person.

The office building was five stories high and had an external staircase that ran along the side of the building. The alarm was always to be set from the top floor. Every evening, I had to set the alarm and use the stairs to walk all the way down to the first floor. From there I used a little alley to walk behind the building and through a side door that led into the basement.

The alarm held a beep for a moment which meant it was set. I started walking down the steel stairs and as I made my way down, sirens echoed out in the distance.

I continued making my way down to the bottom floor when something on the ground caught my gaze. I peered over the side rails and in the alley were three guys, standing, huddled together. One had on a hooded sweater with the hood over his head and the other two wore plain black t-shirts. The only thing I could really see were the tops of their heads.

Great, I thought, *I'm going to get fucking mugged.* A lot of lowlifes live or hang out in Melville. I continued walking down the stairs thinking, *I hope they don't try to mug me, all I have on me is a ten-dollar bill and a Glock 17 tucked into the back of my belt.* The magazine was fully loaded in my back pocket, I could have it inserted into the weapon and ready to fire in seconds. I wasn't stupid; I knew I worked in a bad neighborhood so I always carried protection, even if it was against my parole.

The three figures' heads were fixated on the ground. It seemed as if they were staring at each other's shoes. I took the last step off the staircase and turned, then began walking toward the group, looking straight ahead to prove I was not afraid to walk past them.

As I approached, the three men glanced up and simultaneously gawked in my direction. The one wearing the hood was the first to raise his arms out in front of him, and then the other two followed suit. It seemed as if they were outstretching their arms to reach for something. The three began walking toward me.

I stopped directly under the building's lamp post. The light bulb above illuminated most of the alleyway, but the figures were just outside of the light's glow, I wasn't able to get a good look at their faces. All I could see was the figures shambling toward me.

Great, here they come. I better just say something, I thought.

"Hey guys, how's it going?" I said with as much confidence in my voice as possible.

The strangers made no attempt to communicate; they continued walking toward me. I took a few steps back to keep the distance between us. The man with the hood stepped into the light and I froze when I caught a good glimpse at him. The man's face was completely void of life, his skin was a deathly pale and his eyes were wide open. I thought his eyeballs were going to fall right out of their sockets. A hiss kept gasping out of his mouth like he was having trouble breathing. The hooded man's horrid face will forever haunt me.

The crazed man took a few steps closer so I took a few more back. The other two guys walked into the light. Their bodies formed a human V shape as they walked in pattern. All three had white glossy eyes and their exposed flesh was gray with a tint of purple. There were no friendly expressions on their faces, just a confused, puzzled and anticipatory look. One of them had his mouth wide open while the other two snapped their jaws.

"What the fuck?" I managed to say. I thought they had shot too many drugs and needed help. "Are you guys okay?"

Again there was no answer from any of them. They just kept walking toward me in their slow, staggered movements. I stopped walking back to get a better look at them.

Maybe they were coming to me for help, I thought, but quickly, I learned that stopping to help was a bad idea.

I walked toward hood guy as he continued moving toward me. The man was within reaching distance when he lunged for me. I tried to stagger back but his movements were quick. It shocked the shit out of me. They were moving so slowly and out of nowhere, they sprang to life. He grabbed hold of my arm and tried to bring it up to his mouth. Then, with his other hand, he brought it up and wrapped it around my throat. His hands were cold and felt like I had an ice pack around my neck. I quickly yanked my arm free and shoved my attacker back. He released my throat and fell to the ground. The man bumped into the others as he fell backward. He didn't even try to break his fall, but he did manage to take them down with him. I heard one of their skulls crack as it hit the pavement.

I stopped messing around and drew my weapon. I took the magazine out of my back pocket and inserted it into the pistol. I pointed it at them with my finger around the trigger, not second guessing about firing.

"Stay down," I ordered, but they didn't listen. The men slowly rose to their feet.

"Stop, don't move," I said again, but they still didn't listen. By this point, I was getting very tired repeating myself.

I decided to fire a warning shot into the air to show them I was serious about shooting. My warning shot rang loudly in the little alley; but they didn't even flinch and continued walking toward me. I pointed the weapon back at them. As soon as one of them was close enough to be shot and have it considered self defense ... I fired. The bullet went into the man's stomach. The force of the impact made him take a step back. He didn't fall to the ground like I thought he would. I took a few steps back as blood leaked out of the wound and fired three more shots. One hit the guy in the hood, making contact with his right knee. He dropped to the asphalt but then started crawling toward me, leaving a trail of blood in his wake. The other two bullets met the third man in the chest and blew out of his back, spraying the wall behind him with blood. None of the shots I fired stopped them. They continued walking and crawling toward me.

I put the gun to my side and mumbled softly in disbelief, "I think it's time for me to leave." I have seen some crazy shit in my life, but I have never seen anyone take this many bullets without dropping like a sack of fucking potatoes.

I took the magazine out of the Glock and fired the shot left in the chamber. The bullet went wild; I put the magazine into my pants pocket and holstered the gun back into my waist belt. A Glock 17 doesn't have a safety lock so ejecting the magazine before holstering it will insure I don't accidentally shoot myself. I ran around the group in hopes that I could make it to the parking lot door. At this point, all I wanted to do was get away from these guys. As I ran, I noticed that their eyes never let me out of their sight. They didn't look away once. I made it to the door and turned to take one last look at my attackers only to see them tumble over each other trying to follow me.

The hinges creaked as I yanked the door by its handle and hustled inside. My Maroon 2003 Hyundai Sonata was the only car left in the parking lot. I took the keys out of my pocket and disabled the alarm. At that moment, banging erupted from the door behind me, followed by gargled and air-filled moans. I stared at the door, waiting for it to open. It never did, but the banging continued. I got in my car and turned the ignition.

The tires of my Hyundai peeled out as I hurried toward the shutter doors. As I approached, they slowly began to rise. To my shock, I caught the first glimpse of the devastation that plagued the town of Melville.

Fires blazed wildly out in the distance, woman and children ran wildly as others mauled and attacked the unluckily few who lost balance and fell to the ground. Screams echoed all around as the expressionless folks snapped and nipped at their flesh. I snapped out of my astonishment and quickly made a left turn heading East up Colonial Road.

From my front shirt pocket I pulled out my cell phone and called Stuart. He answered in a calm and relaxed voice, as if nothing was happening. He said was at his house, drinking a beer and watching the basketball game. I told him what I saw, but he didn't believe me. He was in the middle of asking me if I was drunk when the sound of shattering glass crashed in the background.

I heard Stu yell some profanity through the phone's receiver. "Hold on," he said, putting the phone down to investigate the noise. A struggling racket began and I heard Stu's faint voice calling for help.

I screamed into the phone, "I'm on my way," then threw the phone down onto the passenger seat.

There were a lot of people on the street. Most of them looked like the trio I encountered in the back of the office building. Others were either running or being attacked. There were people on top of people, biting and ripping clothes.

A squad car was stopped over the sidewalk as its lights blared red and blue. As my Sonata approached, I saw a police officer on the ground, motionless, next to the cruiser. His clothes were torn to shreds and the bullet proof vest that was intended to protect him was lying by his feet. The pig's stomach was ripped wide open. Blood and half eaten intestines were spewed everywhere around him as if someone, or something, tore out his insides to have a snack. I quickly looked away as I noticed that the dead police officer was slowly trying to rise to his feet.

I was the only moving vehicle on the road. All the other cars were either on the sidewalk or left abandoned on the street. Most of them had their headlights on while others flashed hazard lights. The full moon and blazing wild fires kept the streets well lit. I drove slowly so that I wouldn't hit anyone either running on the road or the expressionless walking in their direction.

I turned the radio on to see if the

news was talking about this.

"... eryone please stay in your homes. Lock the doors and barricade yourselves in. The streets are unsafe. The assailants are physically attacking anyone in their paths. Authorities are on the move and the situation will be handled as soon as possible. Again, please stay in your homes. If you are on the street you will be considered a threat and will be incarcerated."

That's all I got to hear as Stu's house was only a few minutes from my work. Getting out of the car, I reached for the Glock and unhooked it from my belt as the car door swung and shut behind me. The magazine in my pocket still had a few rounds unfired. I ran toward Stu's house, taking the magazine from my pocket and inserting it into the pistol. There were a few of those expressionless outside, but I ran past them. Turning the knob to Stu's front door, I let myself in and slammed the door shut behind me.

"Stu?" I held the pistol out in front of me ready to fire. "Stu?" I yelled again.

The glow from the television screen illuminated the otherwise dark living room. A TV dinner tray sat on top of the coffee table. From the smell of it, I knew it was cardboard steak. One of the most foul smelling things in the world.

"I'm in here." A faint voice responded to my query from the kitchen.

Heading left, I rushed into the

kitchen. Stu was next to the kitchen table, standing over a lifeless body on the titled floor. Stu held a baseball bat with his right hand. A stream of blood conjoined at the tip of the bat and red drops fell to the floor.

"Are you okay?" I asked panicked. "What the hell happened?"

"I don't know," he answered, setting the bat down next to the kitchen counter. "This guy fucking crashed into my sliding glass door. He just walked through it. I ran in and he was face down on the floor. The broken glass cut him up good so I thought he was dead. I was going to call an ambulance, but the fucker just stood up. He looked at me and tried to bite me. We struggled for a bit and I pushed him off. I grabbed my bat and bashed his fuckin' head in. We need to get rid of this body Stanley, I can't go back to prison. Come on, help me, grab his legs. We'll stuff him in my couch and take it to the dump tomorrow."

Stu stood over the man's upper body; he knelt down and reached for the man's shoulders. Stu and I have disposed of a lot of bodies in our past, but today, I didn't think we'd get in trouble for this.

"Stuart," I said, almost yelling, "I don't think it's going to matter. Something's going on outside. I'm not sure what it is but it's somethin' big. We have to get out of here and stay off the streets. The cops are cracking down on anyone outside. We need to make it to my house, your glass door is fucked, we'll be safer there. Go get your guns, we're gonna need them."

"Yeah, okay, but I'm running low on ammo. It's getting harder to come by."

"Don't worry about that, just go get what you have, but hurry, there's more of these people outside." I pointed in the direction of the front door.

Stuart darted out of sight like a ghost. I waited in the kitchen examining the man my brother had killed. He smashed this gray skinned man's head in real good. The top left of his head was nothing but a big open hole, blood and brain matter oozed out. His eyes and mouth were fixed open; his teeth were covered with a thick layer of dried blood. He appeared dead ... really dead. The expressionless I fought in the alley looked like this thing, but they were still moving. I shot them and it didn't have any affect. *Why was this one laying here lifeless when the other ones didn't die when I shot them?*

"Maybe it's the head." The words flew out of my mouth in revelation.

Banging erupted at the front door.

"Stu, hurry up, we have company." I looked away from the body and slowly stood.

Stuart came back into sight carrying two gun cases, one contained his beloved AK-47 and the other, a .357 magnum revolver.

"Here, give me the revolver," I said, putting the Glock on the nearest countertop. "We need to go out the back. Load up the magazines on the AK and leave the rest of the ammo here. I have more at my place. The less we have to carry to my house, the better."

He handed me the small case. I placed it on the table and opened it. The kitchen light reflected off the silver firearm. Also inside the case was a box of rounds. I placed the ammo on the table and took the firearm out of the padded foam. Memories of the gun flashed in my head as I pushed in the cylinder release. The cylinder came out of the gun's frame. I took some rounds out of the box and inserted them. I gave it a quick spin for good luck and slapped it back into place.

I watched Stu as he loaded cartridges into the magazine of the AK. Thoughts of our criminal days kept running in my head. The last time I saw him load an AK we were about to rob the Melville bank. Stu was caught by the pigs that day; I ran into the woods and was able to get away. Stu though, went to prison for five years. I was caught a year later, but only got two years in prison. After we both got out, we decided to go straight, but we still love playing with guns. It took us a few months, but we found Stu another AK that was just like the one taken away from the cops. He was thrilled.

"All right, Stan let's go." Stu put one of the magazines into the assault rifle and shoved the rest into the front pocket of his sweater.

I grabbed a few more rounds for the
.357 and put them in my shirt's front
pocket. I reached for the Glock with my
right hand; leaving the .357 in my left.
The safety was off on the Magnum so it was
time to go. I may have played strong in
front of Stu, but I was deathly terrified,
I didn't want to go back out there but we
had to. My house would be safer until we
could figure out what was going on.

Here I go again, I thought, *stepping
into a world gone mad.*

Stu had the bigger weapon so he took
point, I followed closely behind him. We
made our way around the house. There were
six of them, all banging on the front door
trying to gain entrance. My car was directly behind them parked over the sidewalk and on Stu's lawn. We ran in that direction, trying not to make eye contact
with them.

We made it inside and I started the engine. The loud roar brought attention to
us. All six turned and looked in our direction.

"They look dead, don't they?" Stu
asked. "Kind of like they're zombies."

"Don't be stupid, Stu." I put the car
into drive and stepped on the accelerator.
"We don't know what the hell is going on.
It could be mass hysteria or whatever the
fuck they call it."

Stu went quiet and stared off into the
decimated streets. Not too many people
were on the streets now, cars were everywhere though. I had to swerve around them.

36

We were the only ones moving and everyone stared in our direction. All of them had that same expressionless look of dead as those I'd encountered earlier that evening.

The drive was uneventful. We made it to my house with no trouble. I parked in the driveway and turned the car off. We got out and looked around the small neighborhood. Everything seemed normal, but with all the shit happening tonight, I didn't trust the silence. We walked to my front door when we saw one. He was turning the corner of my house. I had no idea what he was doing there or how he got there, but he was walking toward us. My trash cans were in his path but he didn't pay any attention to them. He continued walking, knocking over the cans and spilling garbage on my yard.

Stu tugged on my arm and said, "You think we're not dealing with zombies? I'll show you."

He turned to face the man again and raised the weapon to his shoulder. The AK roared as he unloaded the entire magazine into the expressionless. It stopped him dead in his tracks as each bullet ripped though his gray flesh. The man fell and landed with a loud thud as he hit the ground. Blood poured out of the holes in his body.

What a waste of ammo, I thought.

I might have punched Stu if I didn't have over a thousand rounds for the AK in my house.

We waited for a matter of seconds to see if the expressionless would rise again. I thought I'd hear someone yell that they were going to call the cops. We didn't hear anything, just silence, and the man started moving again. He sat up and stared in our direction. I don't know why I didn't believe Stu. I've seen this happen before. I shot three and they kept coming. I guess I was just tired of my big brother always being right.

The man stood to his feet with blood still exiting from the bullet holes. His clothes were tattered and what was left of his flesh was exposed. I pulled the hammer back on the revolver and walked up to the man.

"Well if they *are* zombies," I said as I raised the gun to the man's head, "then this will stop him." I pulled the trigger as the expressionless thrashed its arms towards me. The bullet went through his left eye socket. A sickening noise erupted from the back of his head as the bullet exploded out leaving a baseball-sized hole. Brain matter and blood flew out the gaping hole. The man fell back onto the ground and didn't move.

We didn't say anything to each other. We finished walking to the front door. I took the keys out of my pocket, unlocked the door and walked in.

My house was always dark, I love my privacy. I flicked the light switch on and closed the door behind Stu. Immediately we barracked ourselves inside, and then headed for the master bedroom to wait for the news.

* * *

I snap out of my daze when Stu starts flipping through the television channels.

All of the regular programming is on. I would have thought that in a disaster like this, the news would be on every channel. It doesn't even seem like anything is going on. There is always a news update at eight, that's what we're waiting for.

I lean back in my chair again and continue waiting. I close my eyes when an all too familiar tune begins to play. The news update is starting so I sit up and anticipate the information.

"Hello and good evening, I'm Glen Sanders bringing you your eight o'clock news update. Breaking news ... police reports confirm that the town of Melville has been overrun by assailants said to be infected with a virus known as Hemagglu-A. This virus has spread twenty miles within the past four hours. The infected seem dazed and unwilling to reason. They are hostile and should be avoided at all costs. New reports suggest that the infected are ..."

Glen pauses, holding his right ear. He looks to his left and speaks into the earpiece.

"Is this correct? Has this been confirmed? I'm not saying this to the public if it's ..."

He pauses.

"Okay, yes, I understand."

Glen looks back to the video camera and addresses the viewing public.

"New reports confirm that the infected are ... the recently deceased coming back to life and attacking the living. This has been confirmed and re-confirmed by experts and many other news stations. It is true; the infected are in fact the living dead. I know this is hard to believe, but denial may cost you your life."

* * *

"I told you!" Stu yells. There's no reason to yell, I'm only a few feet away.

"Shhh," I respond turning back to watch the news cast.

* * *

"Dr. Thomas Blakeman, an expert in the field of viral epidemics, is standing by to answer a few questions. Dr. Blakeman can you hear me?"

The screen splits in two, one side is a headshot of Glen and the other of the doctor.

"Yes, I can hear you Glen; just Thomas would be fine. Please continue."

"Welcome Thomas, thank you for joining us on this bizarre story."

"Thank you for having me."

"What can you tell us about Hemagglu-A?"

"Well Glen, Hemagglu-A is a blood disease that stops your body from creating

40

new white cells. Once you're infected with Hemagglu-A the human body shuts down completely. The immune system is none existent and the body could die from a simple sore throat. The tests we have conducted after the first cadaver stood up in the Crystal Springs morgue shows that Hemagglu-A is not the cause. In all honesty we do not know what is causing the dead to rise."

"This is unbelievable. You said Patient Zero, the first known carrier of the disease, was in the Crystal Springs morgue? Do you know how the infection spread into the nearby towns?"

"We believe that the cadaver in Crystal Springs was not Patient Zero. This was just the first time I came into contact with one of the infected. My colleagues and I studied the subject behind a glass window. No one wanted to be around the infected male."

"Was the patient hostile from the beginning?"

"Yes. His eyes opened a little after the nurse wheeled him into the morgue. The sudden act of movement shocked the nurse causing her she leap away. After composing herself she began feeling his neck for a pulse. That's when the infected male attacked. I was not there when this assault took place, but the nurse reported to the authorities that his eyes opened and attacked her like a vicious animal, biting into her forearm and tearing away a chunk of flesh. The man proceeded to consume the piece of tissue he snagged. The nurse later became ill while getting treated for the bite she suffered in the attack."

"Excuse me, did you say he consumed her flesh?"

"Yes, the cadaver bit into her forearm and managed to take a hunk of flesh. He continued to chew and swallow. We cannot be one-hundred percent sure if this is what happened but all the evidence shows this is true."

"What would cause someone to become a cannibal?"

"Like I said, we do not know. I can only inform you of what we have observed."

"What was the infected male doing while you observed him?"

"He was doing nothing. He stood in a corner and stayed there the entire time. Only when one of the police officers was sent in to bond the cadaver, did he move. It was very hard for the police officer to get a grip on him so the first attempt was a failure. The infected male struggled with the police officer, trying to bite any piece of exposed flesh. On the second attempt, the officer managed to cuff the infected male, and then bonded him to a metal slab table. Once the patient was subdued we began our experiments. He was, in fact, dead. There was no heartbeat, no blood pressure, there was nothing. His eyes were glazed over with a thin layer of a white cloudy substance. The entire time his mouth snapped at us, trying to bite anyone who got close."

"Fascinating. Thomas I am being told that we must move on and we should have you back on if any new information is available. Is there any final comment you would like to inform us with?"

"Yes, Glen, I will join my colleagues for our next experiment with the cadaver. The only advice I can give you is do not make any contact with the infected. The virus is one-hundred percent fatal. All who are infected will come back to life and attack the living."

"Thank you, Thomas, please keep us posted." The screen flashes and goes back to Glen, who shuffles papers around the news desk. He looks back into the camera. "Thank you for joining us this has been your eight o'clock news update. Please join us again for your news update at nine. I'm Glen Sanders."

* * *

Regular programming returns to the screen. I'd be watching *Two and a Half Men* right now but we have work to do. I look over to Stu, he's sitting on the corner of my bed with an indescribable facial expression. I can't believe this is really happening. Everything was so normal this morning. I got up and went to work, I got off of work and the world turned to shit. I hate how the news station doesn't give you any useful information. All they can do is tell you to stay home. What about when the infection reaches my front door. What the fuck are we going to do then?

"Hey Stu," I say getting up from the bed and heading out the door. "Get up and let's go get the rest of my ammo."

In my spare time I created some hidden closets around the house, you never know when the cops will surround the place. I use some to hold ammo and anything else I don't want people to find.

We walk to each closet and take everything we can back to the bedroom and set the ammo on the bed. I start loading a magazine for the Glock. I look behind me and Stu is walking in the door with the rest of the ammo.

"Is that everything?" I ask.

"Yeah. What do you think is going to happen?"

"To what, life?"

"Yeah," he says with a nervous tone, "if this is as bad as what the news says then where are we going to go? What are we going to do? Fight our way out of town?"

"Look Stu, I have no idea what we're going to do. I think we're just going to stay here and if something comes up we'll grab our shit and head out. We know how to stop these fuckers if they get in our way. It's only us. We have no one else to worry about."

"Well don't you think we should—"

We interrupt your regular scheduled programming to bring you this special news update ...

"This hour just flew by, wait ..." I look at my watch, "it's only been half an

44

hour. Something must be going on. Stu turn it up."

* * *

"This is Glen Sanders with an urgent news update. Chaos and horror is now sweeping the nation as the unknown virus spreads across the United States. We have confirmed reports of the dead rising from as far as the Utah boarder. We have again Thomas Blakeman with us to explain what they have learned. Thomas?"

The screen splits and both Glen's and Thomas' headshot appears. Thomas looks as colorless as a phantom. Sweat runs down his forehead. He raises his hand in front of his mouth and coughs. The nails on his hand are bright yellow.

"Thomas, are you okay?"

"Yes, Glen, please, let's continue."

"Is there any new information you can give us?"

"Yes Glen. This virus is like nothing we've ever seen. It reanimates dead tissue cells and brings them back to life. This is not to be taken lightly. The infected are dangerous in numbers. They are in fact dead and they seem to only want to do one thing. They want to eat human flesh. We do not know why. The virus is spread through fluidic contact. Bites, scratches or even blood splatter will more than likely infect you. The virus doesn't seem to be airborne so your chances of getting infected staying away from these people are highly unlikely. Best advice we can give to the people is to stay calm, stay at home away from the infected. If someone has been infected, isolate or eliminate them as soon as possible. So far, we know of only one way to stop the infected and that is to destroy the brain.

"So please everyone stay in your home and don't try to seek out loved ones. Board up your windows, barricade your doors and if you have multiple floors destroy the staircase and stay above ground. The infected are not very intelligent and their coordination is limited. None of them have ever been seen jumping or even climbing. They don't notice any of their surroundings unless there is a living person in their presence. This is the best advice we can give you, your local police and the United States Military are working to secure the infected areas."

"Do you know how long it takes for the virus to slay the victim?"

"The nurse that was bitten earlier today expired not to long ago. I was in her room at the time she flat-lined. The nurses and doctor came in with the crash cart when her eyes reopened. The noise from the EKG was still beeping, but she was looking around at everyone. The nurses ran out the door and then the doctor. I leaned in closer to examine her, thinking she was subdued, when she lunged forward and bit into my shoulder. I already feel the effects of the virus spreading through my body."

The screen goes black for a few seconds

and returns with Glen in the newsroom.

"I believe we have just lost our feed with Thomas." Glen says, his voice trembling as he continues, "I hope he's going to be all right." He shuffles papers around looking down at his desk as his hands come into view. He's obviously frightened and can't control his nerves. He looks back into the camera and continues. "The White House has declared a State of Emergency. Marshall Law has just been put into effect in all cities known to be infected. The police are asking all citizens to please stay in your homes until they sort out the situation. President Kepler will be holding a press conference in just a few minutes, but first we have our Field Reporter, Rick Abbott, coming to us *live* from R.C. Park. Rick can you hear me?"

The screen flashes black, when the picture comes back on, Rick is standing next to a sign that reads, "Randi Connelly Memorial Park". A patch of open field is on his right and off in the distance human silhouettes are seen moving in his direction. He has a microphone in his right hand, holding it up to his mouth.

"Yes, Glen I can hear you. I'm standing right outside the R.C. Memorial Park and as you can see behind me, there is a massive amount of infected walking about. They are at a distance so we are safe here for the time being. They are slow and are easy to out-run. They are very quiet so you'll need to watch your back. We have

just witnessed an attack so we are a little jumpy. If you must go outside for any
reason please be armed with a blunt object
such as a crowbar or even a firearm. If
you're being attacked remember, destroy
the brain and don't let the infected bite
or scratch you. Like Dr. Blakeman said we
urge everyone to stay home and stay above
ground. If you have an abundance of sup-
plies please take them with you. There is
no way of knowing how long this threat
will last, but looking at the number of
infected ... it's not looking good."

The infected continue to close the gap
between them and Rick.

"They are getting closer so we better
get out of here," a very faint voice says
over Rick's voice as he continues talking
about the infected. Rick stops talking and
looks behind him. The horde of undead have
tripled since he last looked in their direction.

"Oh sh(bleep)! Let's go!"

The camera does not turn off and is
dropped to the cameraman's side. The camera is pointed towards the infected closing in. Rick and the cameraman run back to
the news station van, the camera bumps up
and down as they move. The cameraman trips
and falls over a rock placed in the middle
of a grass patch. The camera lands on the
perfect angle to get a back view of the
infected heading towards him.

"Ow, my leg," the cameraman yells out
in pain.

He tries to get back up ignoring the

pain, but falls down again. As he lands, the side of his head hits a watermelon sized rock. Blood immediately begins running down his face as his mouth drops open in surprise. Rick backtracks and helps him up, but his body is limp. The cameraman looks to be going into shock and as the infected get closer, Rick begins to panic. He drops the cameraman realizing that blood has covered his clothes. He looks at the blood on his hands and says, "I'm sorry."

Rick looks into the camera and picks it up. He spins the camera around to look behind him. The infected are a few feet away now, their eyes fixated on the cameraman lying helpless on the ground. Rick runs, only taking a few steps when he stops and looks behind him again, the dead surround the cameraman. All of them kneel down and rip into his flesh. The expressionless claw, bite and rip apart any piece of exposed flesh. Each infected bring chunks of flesh to their mouth and chew. The camera continues recording the mayhem for a few more seconds before Rick turns it and runs. The screen goes black.

The picture does not return for a matter of seconds. Glen comes back into view, sitting behind the news-desk.

"Rick? I believe we've lost Rick. Sorry you had to see that. Our hearts and prayers go out to the cameramen's family." He sighs. "Please understand it is dangerous to go outside and casualties will happen if you're not careful."

A look of shock washes over Glen's face.

"WHAT?" he yells into his earpiece. "Has this been confirmed?" Another long sigh leaves his mouth. Sweat is clearly visible falling down his forehead. He loosens his necktie and unbuttons the top of his collared shirt then stares back into the camera. You could almost feel the hurt in his voice.

"We have just been informed that the President and most of his staff have passed away a few moments ago. Details are obscure but it's being reported that the President was infected earlier today. He expired minutes ago as he was preparing to address the nation. Shortly after his death, the Commander in Chief rose to attack his staff. The Secretary of Defense, the Joint Chiefs of Staff, the First Lady and more of the presidential staff were in attendance. The secret service had strict orders to eliminate anyone infected, which included the President himself. This is by far the darkest day in American history.

"Vice President James Baker has taken the responsibilities of Commander-in-Chief and there is no word on when he will address the nation. We have to ..."

The television went completely dark. We stare into the darkened screen waiting for something to happen.

"The President, Bro," Stu says, breaking the silence. "He just took out his own people. Well, that's what they're saying anyway."

"Yeah, I can't believe it. Society is falling apart fast. What do you want to do?"

Stu pauses, and then gives a malicious smile. "I want to kill all of these fuckers. One of them broke my damn glass door. Maybe we can take care of all of them and things will go back to normal. I hate having guns with nothing to shoot but now ... we can shoot these things without worrying about the cops."

I smile at my brother's attempt to hide the fact that he's terrified. "All right, let's just stay here until we know more of what we're dealing with. Hopefully the news will come back on ... with all this shit happening I bet they're having technical difficulties."

"Or maybe it's your stupid ass old TV," Stu utters as he walks up to the TV. "I'll fix it." He begins playing with the cables.

"I don't know, I think it's the network, Stu."

"Are you sure?" Stu asks as he continues pushing cables.

"Yeah just go to another channel and see if you get a picture."

Stu pushes the button and the channel changes. Most stations have mindless commercials on with black text rolling at the bottom of the screen that reads:

Attention: President Kepler dead, Vice President Baker will address the nation. Streets are unsafe. Please stay in your homes. We are in a State of Emergency. Re-

*main calm, stay tuned for further instruc-
tions.*

"Go back to channel five." Stu turns the channel but the screen is still black. "Just leave it there; hopefully they'll come back in a little bit."

A few seconds pass and the screen flickers as a black and white helicopter view of the city emerges out of the darkness. There is no sound and it's hard to distinguish what we are seeing. A crowd of about fifteen expressionless circle a group of four citizens.

Fire out from gun muzzles appears every few seconds. With every gun flash one of the infected falls to the ground. The picture stays on the group until all of their attackers have been brought down.

The camera looks as if it's about to pan out, when one of the fallen infected explodes. A few seconds later, another detonates followed by another. Each time an infected explodes it sprays the group with contaminated blood. The camera shakes with every explosion.

After the last infected on the screen explodes, the group on the ground is motionless. Minutes pass and one by one, the group stands up and begins walking in that familiar infected march. The screen flickers again and goes dark.

I look down and notice I still have rounds and a magazine in my hands. I'm standing next to the bed trying to make sense of everything I just saw.

"WHAT THE FUCK WAS THAT?!" Stu yells.

I motion for him to keep his voice down and say, "I have no fucking clue; it looked like they exploded once they were brought down. Maybe it's a counter-attack?"

"Yeah, right, like the Predator after Arnold kicked his ass?" Stu spat back sarcastically.

"I suppose," I reply trying to keep calm. "The one I shot outside didn't explode. Maybe it's only some of them?"

"Well how are we supposed to know the difference between them?" Stu asks agitatedly.

"I don't know. We might find out when the news comes back on."

"If it ever does ..." His voice trails off then comes back angrily, "I hate not fucking knowing!"

He throws a round at the television screen.

"Stu, calm down, you're going to break my fucking TV. We'll figure something out. We always do. Remember when we were jumped in the alley of that strip joint?"

Stu smiles as he remembers our past. "Yeah, those fools came out of nowhere. How many did we end up killing?"

"The count was four, and the other three took off running once they saw the knives."

Stu's smile increases in size and says, "Yeah, good times. I miss that knife I wonder whatever happened to it." He begins to shadow fight the air acting as if he has a knife in his hand.

"I don't know, but see? We've been in jams before and always manage to make it out. This shouldn't be any different. Yeah they're dead, but if we're careful we can deal with anything these fuckers throw at us. So stop being a little prissy bitch." I laughed at my joke. Stu does not like being called a bitch. But I do it anyway to get him worked up. He stops shadow fighting and gives me a cold look.

"I'm only fucking with you," I say still laughing. I look back down at my hand and continue loading rounds into the magazine.

"I'm starving," Stu says angrily. "Do you have anything to eat?"

"You mean you didn't have enough to eat with that cardboard steak? Check the fridge and bring me back something too, oh and a beer."

Stu walks out of the room as I place the fully loaded magazine on the bed. I look over my shoulder in the direction of the closet then turn and walk toward it. I slid the closet door out of the way and look for my tactical vest. It hangs on a coat hanger. I bring it out and place it on the bed then take my shirt off and put a clean one on. I put the tactical vest on and begin putting magazines in the pockets.

"STAN!" Stu yells from the hallway at the top of the stairs. I run out of the room with the Glock in my hand in the direction of the yell. I see Stu looking out a window that has a view of the front yard. I run up to him.

"What's up?"

"Look," he replies pointing out the window.

My mouth falls open as I peer out the windows to see hundreds of expressionless outside. The dead are on the streets and on the neighbor's lawn. They came out of nowhere, probably followed my car here.

"It's a good thing we got here when we did," I say.

"Yeah right." A malicious grin washes over Stu's face.

"And we're back, we seemed to have some technical difficulties. Thanks again for joi ..."

"The news cast is on again," I say. We walk back into the bedroom. I stand in front of the television and watch.

* * *

"The images you last saw were from our Channel Five News Chopper. We received the video feed but the coding interrupted our signal. The picture you saw was accidentally streamed to your television.

"We know that obliterating the brain immobilizes the infected. News reports and the images you saw show that the infected will explode seconds after the brain is decimated. Not all infected will explode after being destroyed. Only those who have bright yellow skin color. We do not understand why they are doing this, but avoid destroying the yellow skinned infected."

Glen clears his throat and continues.

"We all have seen what has been going on in the streets these last few hours. This is nothing like we've ever seen. We have just received word that the epidemic has spread to all of the forty eight home states. No new reports are coming from Hawaii or Alaska. We can only hope there's no disturbance. News updates from New York, Massachusetts and Florida have stopped coming in. We believe it to be a technical difficulty but there is no answer from telephones, landlines or mobile. We did receive this video before our connection was lost. Please be advised this tape is highly graphic."

The screen goes blank and a very bad quality cell phone video begins playing. A party is underway with underage teenagers walking and dancing in front of the camera. Bottles of Corona and Captain Morgan are in view. One kid looks into the camera and screams, "I can't feel my legs!"

The camera shies away from that kid.

"Idiot," someone says in a soft voice over the music. A group of teenagers are circled around a shirtless teenage male. A red mark is clearly seen on the left side of his stomach.

"Hey guys check this out." He points to the person taking the video. "You too Chris, bring your big ass over here."

"Steve, put your shirt back on; you're scaring the girls away. We don't have enough alcohol to make you look good."

They both laugh at the joke. The camera

56

bounces up and down as the laughter continues.

"All right, check this out. You're recording right?"

"Yeah, yeah just go already."

Steve stands on top of a table and jumps into the air. He twists his body mid air doing a back flip, but doesn't spin all the way and comes crashing down to the floor. The crowd awes when his head makes contact with the wooden floor boards. The sound of bone breaking echoes in the air. The crowd pauses, then laugher erupts, even the cameraman laughs, bouncing the camera as he snorts. Steve's body lays there motionless.

A female voice in the crowd says, "Guys, shut up." The teens quiet as the girl continues, "I think he's hurt, we better call an ambulance." She kneels down to check a pulse.

Another person in the crowd yells, "Where's Derrick? It's his house, tell him to call."

The camera moves around the room full of panicked teens. With every person Chris runs into, he asks, "Have you seen Derrick?"

Chris walks into a bedroom and notices a body standing in a corner. His back is to the camera.

"Hey Derrick, we have a problem over here, come look."

There is no answer, Derrick's arms reach up to his mouth.

"Derrick ... hey! What the hell are you

doing?" Chris asks.

Derrick slowly looks behind him with gray glossy eyes and his mouth is covered in blood. The camera moves away as Chris takes a big step back. Derrick turns his entire body revealing his stomach wide open and his entrails dangle out. In his hand, he has a piece of his large intestine. Derrick drops his snack; a loud smack echoes as it hits the floor. Derrick walks toward the camera.

"Jesus (bleep)ing Christ!"

Chris runs back to the room where the accident happened, the camera bouncing along as he runs. The camera moves from left to right, no one is in sight. The camera looks down to where Steve's body laid but it is gone, replaced by a pool of blood with a human imprint. Screaming begins as the camera looks towards the back door. To the left side of the screen the figure of a man is seen moving slowly toward the back door. Chris moves the camera towards the figure. It's Steve; his head is drooped down the side of his body. It doesn't look like his spinal cord is intact. A moan erupts behind the camera. Chris turns around as Derrick reaches for him. The camera drops to the floor and gets kicked in to a corner. The lights dim as a painful cry echoes in the background.

* * *

The screen flashes and returns to Glen. The coat from his suit is gone, along with his red tie. His light blue shirt is fully unbuttoned exposing a bleach white undershirt. The camera is no longer steady, there's a lot of background noise, people talking and loud footsteps. Glenn is looking toward the camera but his head is tilted down. His hand is up to his ear trying to listen to his earpiece.

"What do you mean they're inside the building ...?" He pauses to listen. "All of them?" His nerves show as his hand began to shake. "Cut it short? But I have about thirty minutes worth of material. I can't get all this information out before we ..."

Again he listens to the voice in the earpiece.

A shaky voice from the background says, "Glen you're on!"

Glen looks back into the camera. His eyes are blood shot. He's breathing heavily and sweat continues to fall down his forehead. He holds a white page in front of him. The page is shaking in his hand. He swallows and then continues.

"Please forgive the interruption. It appears that the infected outside our building have broken through our barricade and are now inside the Channel 5 News building. I will have enough time to get this information out to you then I'll proceed to the bomb shelter where the Channel 5 News employees will hold up. There are four military protected zones in our county. They offer food, water and protection to anyone looking for refuge. The military is also asking that any able man ages eighteen to thirty-five to please show up ready to be armed and join the fight. Man-power is running short and it is becoming harder to hold off the increasing number of infected. Upon arrival please be ready to give a blood sample followed by a quick cheek swab. No one infected will be let in through the gates. If there is an infected person in your party they will be shot on sight and burned.

"If there are any loved ones already infected, leave them behind as it is al-ready too late for them. Any extra sup-plies you can bring will be welcomed, food, water, medical supplies etc. Please look at the bottom of the screen for the locations of the four safe zones."

White text appears at the bottom of the screen that reads '4565 Catty Road, Ocean-side ---- 79960 Wilkins Street, Rainbow ---- 940 Sonic Avenue, Escondido ---- 86753 Solar Avenue, Cedar.'

Glen continues, his speech moving fast-er, "The safe zones are visible from the addresses given below. A copy of the loca-tions has been posted on the Channel 5 News website. Up-to-date news and informa-tion will also be available there. As of now the Internet is the only reliable source of information. Most television channels have already turned to the Emer-gency Broadcasting System. We here at Channel 5 News must log off now and every-one please stay safe. I'm Glen San ..."

The sound of heavy doors swigging open

interrupts Glen. A combination of moans and desperate cries surround the newsroom. Individual employees run across the camera followed by a group of people that push their way through the field of the camera. Glen looks at the forming crowd, finds an opening, and jumps over the news desk to join the running swarm. The camera tilts down as the man holding it lets go and begins to run. The moans are increasingly louder now. Feet are seen shuffling in front of the camera and then the screen turns to the Emergency Broadcasting System.

Stu and I both stare into the TV dumbfounded.

I break the silence. "So what do you want to do now? Wanna head for the safe zones? Maybe we can help."

"Sounds good to me." Stu takes a sip from his beer. "How are we going to make it over there? Did you see how many of them are out there now?"

I smile. "We're going to fight our way there. It should be fun."

I check under my bed and find a long red case. I pull it out and place it on the bed next to the rest of the firearms and ammunition. I open the case and there is my Remington 870 Police. I've always felt a connection with this shotgun. It might have been all those times it scared someone out of my house. I love the power it brings, this 12 gauge pump action shotgun will blow someone's head clear off. Next to the shotgun is a box with thirty shells in it. I pull the gun out and begin loading the shells.

On occasion, my house has a lot of un-wanted visitors. I want this gun close to me as much as I can. It's a legal weapon to have so I didn't feel the need to store it in a closet with the rest of my ammo.

I finish loading the shells and look over to Stu who is putting on his tactical vest. No idea where it came from, but he likes to leave things in my house. I hand him the .357 and give him all the rounds I have. He checks to make sure it's loaded and holsters it. He puts some extra rounds in his pocket and gives me the thumbs up.

All of our weapons are loaded and we have as much ammo on us as we can carry. I look through my bedroom window. The ex-pressionless are in my backyard, as well as the front. If we're going to get out of my house we'll have to go through them. I turn back and Stu is finishing up his beer. I grab mine off the counter and fin-ish it as well. I drop the bottle on the bed and turn to Stu.

"You ready, Bro?"

Stu laughs. "I'm ready when you are. I told you they were zombies."

Yeah, yeah, I think.

"There's a lot of them out there, just remember to aim for the head. Try not to get too close to them either. I don't want you getting bitten. Better yet, here ..." I walk to the closet and look for some-thing. "Put this leather jacket on over your vest." I throw it to him. "Just leave it unzipped so you can get to the magazine in the front of the vest."

I turn back to the closet and grab another jacket. I put it on and adjust the vest. If I'm going to be running I want to be comfortable.

"What safe zone are we going for?" Stu asks.

"Cedar is the next town over; it's about three miles from here. There's too many of them out there, we can't take my car. It's about an hour walk. I have a feeling it'll take us longer than that."

"Well alright!" Stu says enthusiastically. "Let's start heading out, my trigger finger is itching."

I grab the Remington off the bed and give it one last check. Stu does the same with the AK.

"Let's go," I say. We walk out of the room and head downstairs. We can hear them walking around outside. Some have started banging on the sides of the house. We make it to the front door and start moving the furniture out of the way. Banging begins on the front door. It only sounds like one of them is right outside the door. I look over to Stu who has the AK on his shoulder ready to fire. I put my hand on the door knob. Stu gives me a nod in agreement.

I swing the door open and Stu unloads a few rounds at the gray skinned zombie banging on the entrance. The body falls to the ground and Stu takes a few steps through the door. I look down at the corpse and see the bullet hole in its head. Dark red blood oozes out slowly and lands on my welcome mat.

"Fucking Stu," I mumble.

I follow Stu out the door, stepping over the fallen corpse. I stand next to Stu and look out into the dead world. The scene is unbelievable, every infected body outside is staring in our direction. I see fire out in the distance, in front of us, over the neighbors' houses. A helicopter flies overhead in the direction of the flames. There's hundreds of expressionless just in my field of vision.

Stu gives me a nudge. "let's go. Don't shoot the yellow ones."

We both raise our weapons to the horde closing in. Stu's AK roars to life and bullets pierce the bodies of the infected. I pump my Remington and blast into the crowd. Bodies fall all around us; a moan creeps up from behind the open door. I turn and shoot at the expressionless male in my house. His head explodes. I pump the shotgun and the empty casing falls to the floor. I look behind the infected man I had just decapitated and see a large horde of expressionless making their way through the house and in our direction.

The infected are all around, there's no where we can go, but to stay here and hold our ground. Stu turns around to load another magazine into the AK. He looks inside the house.

"Fuck!" He groans as he notices that we are completely surrounded.

I fire a few more shots into the mob,

trying to keep them at a distance. It doesn't seem to work. More just show up in their place. We keep firing knowing that we are about to be completely overrun by the expressionless.

Author Note:

A Kid Named, Layne ... I honestly don't remember what I was thinking when I wrote this story. It was suppose to be for an anthology published by Living Dead Press. The premise was, "Children surviving the zombie apocalypse." So, I wrote this story and submitted it. It was accepted to the anthology and I got the contract. I looked it over carefully and I didn't like what it said. I told the publisher I was declining and wanted my story to go elsewhere. I received an e-mail a few hours later saying that my story was rejected. Very mature ... but now, my story is available here.

A Kid Named Layne

"Layne? Layne!" I hear Carrie, my stepmother, yell from outside the bedroom door.

"What, Mom?" I answer back as I stuff more clothes into my backpack.

"Hurry up and take only what's important. Don't forget your toothbrush."

The dead people are coming back to life and she's worried about my toothbrush. This has been happening for a few days now, the dead walking thing.

I overheard Carrie and dad talking about it yesterday morning. I was getting ready for school; it was my first day of sixth grade. I walked into the kitchen when they said something about it being just like the movies. I was never allowed to watch any zombie movies, so I didn't know what they meant.

"Layne? Are you listening to me?" Carrie asks, bringing me back to reality.

"Yes, mom," I answer while I walk to my dresser and reach for my electric Transformers toothbrush which stands at attention. My step-mom walks into my room as I grab the toothbrush and throws it into my bag.

"Your father is waiting downstairs. He's going to take us to your Aunt Kelly's house until things calm down. Do you have clean socks in your bag?"

"Yes, mom," I say in an irritated voice. I hate it when she bugs me like this. I'm not a little kid anymore and I'd really wish she'd stop treating me like one. I'm ten now and she's still treating me like I'm nine.

"Okay then. Give me your backpack and head downstairs; tell your father to get the car running."

I hand Carrie my bag and she grabs it. The first thing she does is open it and checks my packing job. I roll my eyes and walk out the door. She really irritates me. I wish a zombie would eat her; maybe then, she'll leave me alone.

I stroll to the stairs and walk slowly down the carpeted steps. My parents have been telling me that we need to be very quiet. If one of the dead hears us in the house, it'll start knocking on the doors or something and attract more attention. I am too busy with my wristwatch; I'm not paying much attention to my parents.

At the bottom of the stairs, I look around me. The house is really dirty. There are slabs of wood nailed to the windows and there's sawdust everywhere.

Last night, my dad nailed the doors and windows shut. The only door not secure is the one that leads into the garage.

My dad is in there tying stuff to the roof of the SUV. "Hey, Squirt," dad says as he notices me standing at the doorway. "Are you ready to get the heck out of here?"

"I am," I say with a smile and then

frown. "Carrie told me to tell you to get the car started."

He laughs and says, "Yeah, and have them zombies hear us before we even get onto the driveway? She's crazy."

I laugh when I hear my dad call Carrie crazy. She really is. Even though she's not my real mom, I still have to play the role. I only call her 'Mom' when she's around. If I don't call her mom, she starts nagging me. It gets very irritating.

My dad walks to the driver side door and opens it. "Come on, Squirt, get in the back. I need your help with something."

I walk into the garage and open the back car door. On the seat, I see my dad's guns, all of them. The barrels point in my direction and on the floor next to them are a few boxes of ammunition. I am no stranger to guns. I have been shooting since I was a little kid. I am not scared of guns like most kids in my school.

My dad looks over the seat as I climb into the car. "Remember the first rule about firearms?" he asks.

"Yeah," I answer, "a gun is not a toy."

"Good boy, and number two?"

"Always remember that gun safety is important. It will save you from getting hurt," I say in a slow and robotic voice.

He grinds his teeth and says, "A little sketchy but you got the general idea down. Do you remember the firearm safety courses that we took?"

"Yeah, Dad, I remember everything."

"Great. Now pick up the handgun you want to use and load it."

My eyes light up when he says to grab a gun. I check the back seat for the gun that I want. I pick up the .357 Magnum Revolver and push the cylinder release button. I search through the ammo for some rounds.

My dad looks back toward me and notices which gun I have. "Wow, sorry, Squirt, I know I said to pick the gun you want but that .357 is too powerful for you. Hand it to me and pick one of the Glocks. They will be less powerful but will still do damage if someone or something tries to hurt you."

I don't argue with my dad. He is my hero and I love him to death. He has been my best friend all my life and I know I'm his best friend too.

"Sorry, dad," I say to him. "I just wanted the .357 because we have more rounds for it. I didn't go for a Glock because there is no safety button, but if you think a Glock will be the best for me, then that's what I'll take." I put the .357 back on the seat and grab a Glock. There is a holster next to it so I grab it as well. A magazine is already in place so I eject it and notice no rounds have been loaded. I look around for the right cartridges and begin loading the magazine.

"You always amaze me, Squirt. When you're done, load the rest of the guns and make sure the safeties are on. I'm going to check on Carrie." He gets out of the car and heads off to find Carrie.

As he leaves, I holster the Glock and tie the belt around my waist. I start loading shells into the shotgun then work my way to the smaller firearms. I figure he will only be a few minutes.

It takes me twenty minutes to load all the guns. I start to wonder where my dad is. I haven't heard any noises or anything. Maybe he and Carrie are fighting again. They have been doing that for a few days now. When they start arguing, I go to my room and ignore them. However, it's kind of hard to ignore them now that the dead people are walking around the streets.

I continue to worry and think that maybe one of the dead people got in and attacked them. I jump out of the car and run through the garage door into the house. I turn left to the stairs and sprint as fast as I can to the top.

"Dad!" I yell, "Carrie? I mean, Mom? What's taking so long?"

I wait for an answer, but it never comes. I head for my bedroom. That was the last place I saw Carrie, she was checking my bag to see if ...

My backpack is lying on the ground. All of my clothes are scattered around it. I feel emptiness in my chest as I panic. I run throughout the house and yell for my dad, but there is no answer. I begin to cry as I walk down the stairs. I make my way to the kitchen. Tears run down my cheek and I taste a salty flavor when they fall into my mouth. I sit on a chair in the dining room table and put my head on the wood. I continue to sob and wonder where my daddy is, why he and Carrie just left me.

I think about my dad. He always told me to be a man and find solutions to problems. His lectures echo in my head and I calm down. I can't see my face, but I know my eyes are red. I wipe my tears away. I stand up from the chair and walk back into the garage. I look in the ignition and see that my dad left the keys there.

"Laaaaaaayne." A voice suddenly cries from the other side of the garage door.

"Laaaaaaayne," the voice comes again.

It's my dad.

I jump out of the car and run as fast as I can into the house and up the stairs. I hustle into dad and Carrie's room. The door is closed, so I didn't think to check for them in there earlier. I grab the handle and swing the door open. The room is a bloody mess. Red marks are splattered across the carpet and on the walls. But more to my horror, I find Carrie standing next to the bed. She is covered in blood and a large knife is clenched in her hand.

"Laaaaaaayne," the cry comes again.

I know that I'm not an adult, but I know Carrie is crazy and understand what's going on here. Carrie stabbed my Dad and pushed him out the window. I can't see him but I know he's down there calling out for me. I need to get to him before the dead

74

people do. Carrie looks toward me. I feel chills when her crazy eyes meet mine. I don't think twice about pulling the gun out of the holster. She walks toward me with the knife still in her hands.

"You're my son, Layne. I was the one who always took care of you. I was the one who fed you. How could you do this to me?"

I point the gun to her and ask, "What are you talking about crazy Carrie?"

"Don't call me that!" she snaps back and then lunges for me.

I feel the blood rush away from my face as I pull the trigger. Everything feels like it is in slow motion. The muzzle flashes and it is then that I see the bullet hit Carrie in the chest. The round goes through her body and splatters blood across the wall behind her. She jumps back like a wild animal and falls to the floor. She lands on her back next to the bed. Her eyes are wide open as blood gushes out of her mouth, she convulses as more and more blood comes rushing out. Her white shirt is eternally stained with my dad's blood as well as hers. I put the gun back in the holster and run for the open window.

I peer out of the giant window that looks onto the front lawn. My dad rests on the ground in a pool of blood. He holds the side of his stomach. I look into his eyes and he stares back.

"Hey squirt," he says, "my back went out and I can't move. Carrie saw the picture of you, me and your real mom in the backpack. She freaked out and came after me."

"Hold on, I'm going to help you into the house," I say.

"No, it's too late. I see them coming for me. Listen, make it to your Aunt Kelly's house." He coughs and blood spews from his mouth, but he continues talking. "Take the SUV and drive just the way I showed you. If any of the zombies come after you shoot them in the head. Don't let anyone in the car and most importantly, don't worry about me. You have to get out of here."

I see the dead people walking slowly toward my dad. They are disgusting. Some of them have dried brown blood all over their clothes. I can even see bite marks on them and others are missing arms. One of them is missing both legs and is still crawling toward my dad.

"NO!" I yell at them.

"Layne don't look!" my dad yells back. "Get out of here!"

I draw my pistol and fire at a dead person. I hit him on the shoulder. He staggers back, and continues to walk toward my dad. I fire another shot, and this one goes through his head. The dead person instantly falls to the ground, like it lost the will to move. Another few come out of the bushes. Again, I fire at them, and try to aim my shots at their heads. They drop to the ground.

A lot of them come out of nowhere. All of the dead people slowly walk toward my dad.

"Layne! Get out of here," my dad yells, but I don't listen.

I fire every shot I have in the magazine, but it doesn't even stop the dead people. They keep coming and there is nothing I can do to save my best friend. I holster the gun and stare at my helpless dad.

"Go," is all he can say before the dead people pile on top of him like football players do when fighting for the ball.

My dad gives out the most horrifying cry I have ever heard. I know one of them finally bit him. For some reason I can't look away. I'm so scared and all I want to do is sit here and cry for my dad. That's just what I do, I cry as my dad is torn apart by the dead. Through my watery eyes I see one of the dead things look up at me and blares a snarl. I hustle away from the window. They know I'm here now. I have to listen to my dad and get to my Aunt Kelly's house.

I walk toward the door and just before I step out into the hallway, Carrie, my step-mom, sits up. She has turned into one of the dead things. Her eyes are a glossy shade of white. Blood is still pouring out of her mouth and it drips onto her clothing. She looks at me and lets out a horrible air filled hiss. The dead thing that used to be Carrie stands to its feet, more blood gushes out of the bullet hole in her chest. She raises her arms in front of her and walks toward me. I slam the door shut.

I run down the hall and into my bedroom. I collect my clothes and everything else that was in my bag, and re-pack. I find the picture of my real mom, me and my dad. The photo was taken just a few days before the car accident. I need to hurry. I put the picture in my pocket and put the backpack over my shoulder.

Carrie bangs on the door. I wonder why she hasn't gone for the doorknob. Were the dead things not able to use something simple like a door handle? I ignore the banging and hurry down the stairs. I run into the kitchen and grab a few bags of chips and a twelve pack of sodas, then head for the garage.

I open the passenger door and throw the soda and chips onto the seat. I look over to the driver side and there is the .357 that I wanted to use. I take the Glock out of the holster and toss it with the rest of the guns. The holster I'm wearing isn't meant for the .357, but I make it fit. I close all the doors and jump into the driver seat. The control for the electric garage is clipped onto the visor. I adjust the seat so I can reach the pedals. I take the .357 out of the holster and place it next to the chips and soda, just in case I need it.

I'm really scared. I'm trying to think about what I just did to Carrie and what happen to my dad. I need to be strong for both of us. My dad wants me safe and getting to my aunt's is a start. I take a deep breath as I push the button for the garage door. The noise is loud and I'm sure it will attract them. I start the car and put it in drive, just the way my dad taught me. The door slowly raises and I see legs on the other side.

When the door is completely up I see a lot of them moving around outside. I move forward into the driveway. I look to my right and see the crowd of dead people eating away at what's left of my dad. I begin to cry, but I stop when a dead person bangs on my window. I turn to see Mr. Peterson, our next door neighbor. His lips are missing and I can see all of his teeth. He presses his face up against the glass and smears saliva all over the window. I reach for the .357, but quickly think against it.

More dead people notice the SUV. One by one they turn in my direction. I press on the accelerator and the car lurches forward. I use the brakes and turn left onto the street. I only went driving with my dad a few times so I'm not sure how to work everything on the car.

I keep a steady pace as I drive through the dead covered city. There are dead people everywhere and they stare in my direction as I drive by. Their gawking is so creepy. They look at me like they're not staring at me, but are looking through me. Most of them have clear white eyes, but others have red eyes. I wish they would stop staring at me.

My Aunt Kelly lives on the other side of town, out in the middle of nowhere to be exact. It should take me half an hour to get there. I remember my dad telling Carrie something about it being safer where the population is low. I guess no one wants to live out in the boonies.

I turn the radio on, but no music plays. There is only talk radio and I hate listening to that stuff. Nothing is more boring than grown ups talking. I turn it off and notice that I am a block away from my school. It looks so abandoned, it's even scarier than when it's full. I'm so glad my dad told me to stay home today.

I stop the car when I get to the front of the school. I don't know why I'm stopping; I guess I just want to look at something familiar, but so different at the same time. It really looks deserted. I sit for a minute and stare out of the passenger side window toward the empty school. A hand knocks the driver side door.

I jump in fright and turn toward the ruckus. It's my fifth grade teacher Mrs. Jones.

"Layne! Is that you?" she asks.

I shake my head: no.

"Layne, it's me your old teacher, Mrs. Jones. Open the door let me in," she pleas, but I don't listen.

Mrs. Jones was always nice to me. I did like her, but my dad told me not to open the door for anybody.

There was this mark on her cheek, like teeth marks. I hear moans coming from the passenger side door. I turn to look. It's a few of my old classmates. There's Joey, Sam, Crystal, and Jessica, we were all in

Mrs. Jones' class in fifth grade. They look like the dead people. Mrs. Jones screams at me to open the door, but I shake my head again. She bangs on the window trying to break it. My dead friends walk toward Mrs. Jones. She bangs on the door again and again, she is too busy trying to get in she doesn't notice the little hands reaching for her.

Mrs. Jones howls in pain as they bite into her shins. She falls back and I stare as my old friends rip her to pieces.

"Sorry Mrs. Jones," I mumble to myself as I put the SUV in drive and speed away.

As I drive through the ruined town, and see all the undead faces staring at me, I get this feeling of disgust. I've lost my dad, Carrie and my classmates have just killed Mrs. Jones. I don't feel anything anymore. I'm not scared or sad, I just feel numb. I don't want to go to my aunt's house. I don't want to do anything. The world around me is ending and I don't want to be here anymore. There's nothing left. I'm sorry dad, but I'm not going to make it to my Aunt Kelly's house.

I stop the car and grab the .357 Magnum.

"I'll see you in heaven, dad," I whisper as I put the gun under my chin and pull the trigger.

UNDEAD
SIDE OF THE MOON

Author Note:

Undead Side of the Moon is the result of a days worth of writing. A friend of mine, Remy Porter, put out a notice to other authors about an anthology of vacation holiday themed zombie stories. I wanted to do something not many people would think of and put my vacation resort on the moon. I think I was on my way to Target when the idea hit me. The following day, I sat down and wrote the first draft. After it came back from my editor, I made revisions and sent it to Wild Wolf Publishing. It was accepted and is in the anthology entitled, *Holiday of the Dead*. It is also found here, of course.

Undead Side of the Moon

To Whom It May Concern:

My name is Elroy Collins and I'm sitting in a prison cell awaiting punishment for what I'm being accused of. I'm writing this to prove my innocence, but the trial is over; I am convicted of murdering my team and every resident at the Moonlit Resort. The only thing left for me to do is to write down my side of the story. Maybe someday, this letter will inform people that the Zilith Corporations was lying.

* * *

We needed to learn to take care of planet Earth before we went off building in outer space. I was against opening the Moonlit Resort for business so soon, but the Zilith Corporation wouldn't listen. Why would they listen to a roughneck like me? I was just head of their secret search and rescue team; no one important.

In 2036 the Zilith Corporation was responsible for the Apophis asteroid impact. By this time, NASA had lost all funding because space exploration was becoming more popular with privately funded organizations. After NASA disbanded, the Zilith Corporation caused an unnecessary public scare, saying that NASA had it wrong and that the asteroid *was* on a collision course with Earth, the United States Government allowed them to shift the asteroid's orbit in order to make the near Earth object hit the moon. It was a successful impact. The entire world watched as Apophis collided with our moon. I was only fifteen years old, but I remember it well. In fact, watching it changed my life. It was at that time that I fell in love with space travel and wanted to do anything I could to become a Space Marshall. The impact made a small explosion on the surface of the moon. A few minutes after the flare-up, dust ejected into space causing a brilliant light show. After the collision was over and the raves to the Zilith Corporation for saving the world stopped, people went back to their lives. Just like the moon landings in 1969. Once the United States beat Russia in the Space Race, people lost interest in the moon.

Five years after the Apophis collision, in 2041, the Zilith Corporation revealed their plan to build a multi-trillion dollar resort on the surface of the moon. Thanks to the asteroid, they had more than enough raw materials waiting for them. The dust still had not settled from the impact, but advances in nano-technology and the space exploration boom of the 2020's, made space walking safer than ever. Not to mention all the scientific breakthroughs of that decade as well. Radiation repelling space suits that could withstand heat greater than 1,000 degrees Fahrenheit made it possible for explorers to go places they'd never gone before, but oxygen levels were still a problem. Zilith was on it, bioengineering artificial lung mechanisms that made breathing in space possible, and they were just a step away from surgically implanting their invention into a handful of human test subjects. Don't ask me about specifics, I'm no scientist. Till this day, I still have not heard of any success stories.

Despite the rough shape the Apophis collision left the moon, Zilith Corporation managed to fully erect the first lunar hotel on the northern part of the moon in only seven years. World scientists agreed it was an ideal location for building, and by 2048, the hotel was completed. Just like with the Apophis collision, people were glued to their E-vision sets as Zilith streamed live video and photos during building construction.

I had been recruited and working security for Zilith nearly two years by the time construction was completed. Zilith is not the type of company you go to find work, if they like your achievements, they find you. I was stunned when a recruiter met me at my graduation. I finished first in my Space Marshall training class and was ready for work. Upon my first day of employment, I had a team ready for me to oversee.

They claimed that no one died in the processes of making the building, but I know the truth. Zilith does a wonderful job keeping everything in the dark. I lost two good friends who were on the moon building project. They hit an air pocket while digging and were ejected into space. The man in charge of the dig told me that before he mysteriously died from natural causes. The official story was that they went insane and killed themselves. Their faces were so badly disfigured that the funeral was closed casket. I'm not sure what they put in those coffins, but it wasn't their remains.

The doors to Moonlit Resort remained closed for the next five years, while Zilith tested the safety and stability of the hotel. When the doors finally opened in 2053, the rooms were fully-booked for the first four years. A one night stay is a flat rate of one-million a head, plus an additional fifty-grand for the lunar shuttle ride each way. Needless to say, the only people traveling to the moon were the wealthy.

Everything was going great until we lost communication with them a few weeks ago. From here on out I will be telling the true story of what really took place.

* * *

We lost communication with the Moonlit Resort on December 28, 2059. The shuttle rides had stopped until we could regain contact. The communications team went to check how the resort was doing, but there was no response. It was dead silent. For an entire week after, they tried to restore communication, but were unsuccessful. The Zilith Corporation kept the lid on tight until more information was known. After many attempts to reach the hotel, my team and I had orders to take an immediate flight to see what happened. I didn't understand it at the time, there was no reason to send armed space officers. There were already security guards at the hotel. I was certain it was just an antenna malfunction and a construction crew could handle it. It wasn't like we received a distress call or anything. We hoped for a simple antenna failure on their end, but we planned for the worst.

"Space Marshal Collins," I heard someone say as I packed my bag with clothing and equipment. I turned and standing in front of me was, Mr. Sam Wallace. He was my direct line to the big wigs at Zilith Corp. If I had something to say to them, I told Mr. Wallace and he relayed the message.

"Sir?" I looked into his dark eyes. His white hair was messier than normal and he looked stressed. His tie was loosened around his neck and the top button of his shirt was undone.

"I have a message for you from the bosses." He paused and took a note out of his inside coat pocket. He handed it to me and said, "That's all and good luck on your venture." He stuck out his hand and we shook.

"Thanks, Sam," I said quite informally as we let go. He turned and walked out of the room.

I opened the message and it read:

Space Marshal Collins

Keep this investigation under wraps. You or your team may not have any contact with family or friends during this mission or until debriefing upon your return. There will be dire consequences if you violate this agreement. Be safe and report back to Mr. Wallace within four Earth days. Thank you for your loyalty to the company.

Zilith Corporation

I put the note in my back pocket and continued packing. I flung the sack over my shoulder and headed toward my team's room.

"Space Marshal. Ten-hut!" Mick said. The four other men in the room quickly stood at attention.

"At ease," I replied. I never liked it when my men greeted me that way. They were not just my men, they were my friends. "Are you guys ready?" I asked, looking around the room.

To the far left was Patrick Swan, the pilot in charge of getting us there and back safely. He stood wringing his hands out in front of him. His sack was closed and sitting on the chair next to him.

Next to Patrick was Mick Greenwell, my second in command and the deadliest shot with an S-801 Rifle. He stared back with his long black hair tied in a ponytail. His sack was closed along with his gun cases.

In the middle, John Megs stood. He was the communications specialist I wanted to take with us in case the antenna needed tweaking. We have taken him with us on different missions to Moonlit Resort. We already considered him part of the team even though, officially, he was not.

Standing to the right, still packing, were the two brothers, Orlando and Austin Flint. Their job was to keep the fire power going in case we were met with an attack.

I looked at Orlando and Austin. "You got five minutes to finish packing. The rest of you head for the spacecraft. John, start your check and get us ready for flight."

The men nodded and filed out of the room.

Spacecrafts were very different than the ones they used pre-2020. Rocket science was also mastered within that decade. The spacecrafts were much smaller and looked like oversized F-16 fighter jets. It took the Apollo missions three days to reach the moon. The Zilith Corp. managed to reach it in approximately 22 hours.

Orlando, Austin and I walked into the spacecraft. John and Mick were already strapped in. Patrick was at the control

91

panels getting the craft ready for flight. I took a seat next to him while Orlando and Austin tied our packs and weapons in the storage containers, then took seats.

The weapons we took to space weren't that different than the ones we used on Earth. Bullets must be exploded out of their casing, but in order for it to fire, there needs to be oxygen present. But there is no oxygen in space. The casings we use are slightly bigger in order to entrap more oxidizer into them. The explosion uses that to fire the bullet. One cool thing about guns is that they will fire faster and better in space than on Earth because there is less atmospheric pressure.

"Mission control this is Shadow Three, copy," Patrick said. "We are ready for flight. Please clear the runway. Over."

There was a pause.

"Copy, Shadow Three, I don't see you on the departure list. Who authorized a space flight for today? Over."

Patrick looked at me and said, "Does anyone know about our mission?"

"Not many," I answered back and took over the microphone. "Mission Control, this is Shadow One, copy? Over."

"Copy Shadow One, who authorized? Over."

"Mission Control, this is a black operation. Contact Sam Wallace if you have a problem. Over," I answered.

There was another pause.

"Shadow One, you're clear for take off.

Clearing runway. Over."

"Thank you, Mission Control. Shadow One over and out," I said.

The other spacecrafts on the runway cleared quickly. There were ten miles of open runway space. I looked back at my team, who were holding on to their seats. Take off was always the worst part about the trip. Seeing those big men terrified of the flight was almost comical.

Patrick began the countdown. "Powering up in three, two, one," he said as he turned on the first thruster. The aircraft began to move forward slowly. "Firing thruster two in three, two, one." He flipped the switch for thruster two. The spacecraft jolted forward at one-hundred miles an hour.

"Ah shit," someone in the back yelled.

I held on to my seat as Patrick began talking again. "Firing thruster three in, three, two, one. Hold on," he said as he pushed the third thruster.

The spacecraft progressed forward near-ly reaching three hundred miles an hour. The runway was running out of space.

Patrick held on to the steering con-trols and yelled, "Here we go!" Pre-2020 spacecrafts were nothing more than a rock-et that moves in one direction. The space-craft we used could be steered, no matter where you were. He pulled back on the han-dles and the spacecraft lifted into the air at three hundred miles an hour. "We're in the air," Patrick said as he put one hand over a red button then continued,

"Turbo thruster in three, two, one." He pushed the red button. The spacecraft bolted forward at the speed of sound and continuously grew to over 25,000 miles an hour. "Wooooooooohooooooo," Patrick yelled as he yanked the steering controls causing the aircraft to spin in circles. At that speed, moving the spacecraft was foolish and deadly.

"Knock it off," I managed to say.

Patrick eased off the spinning and put the spacecraft on course. When the target location was locked, Patrick let go of the steering handles. We blasted through the Earth's atmosphere in seconds. The craft began to calm as we entered space.

I looked back to my team. They took the easy way out and used their gas masks to knock themselves out. Patrick was putting his mask on also. I was the only one in the team who would rather wait twenty-two hours then to have a gas knock me out. Patrick fell asleep almost instantly after putting on the mask. I stayed awake and gawked out of the windows into outer space.

I'd been to space many times before, but just staring out into the amazement never got tiring.

Twenty-one hours passed and I had just woken up from a natural sleep, not a gas induced one. The gas was always set to turn off half hour before arriving at the destination. I decided to wake everyone up before then to give us more time to prepare. Slowly, everyone began to wake up. I

94

was already dressed in my space uniform.

They quickly dressed and began doing a rifle check. Patrick took over the controls and began the landing process. We took our seats as Patrick slowed down the spacecraft. Our estimated time of arrival was in eight minutes.

"Remember," I said, "we're here to see what happened to the communications tower first. If everything looks functional, we move on to the Moonlit Resort. We proceed with caution from there on. There's no telling what we will find, but we always expect the worst. Either the Chinese or terrorists, anything. Stick together." The thrusters shut down and we began descending.

I was able to see the communications tower from the sky. Everything looked fine. Nothing looked destroyed or out of place. There were a few new craters around it but that was normal. The moon was always being struck by small meteorites.

"Patrick, take us down near the tower. We'll trek to the hotel when needed," I said.

Patrick took the spacecraft off autopilot and began landing. We hit the surface with a thud. The craft shook as it settled onto the lunar soil. A clear liquid released from the bottom of the spacecraft sprayed the area around it. The moon's dust sticks to things and would likely cause damage to the craft, this prevented that from happening.

"Grab your gear," I said as everyone

unbuckled.

We grabbed our rifles and masks from the weapons storage container at the craft's rear. The masks strapped around our heads almost like a ski mask. There was a little hose that inserts into our nostrils for air. The hose attaches at the bottom to a small tank, no bigger than a spray paint can. The oxygen in those containers would last twenty-four hours. The masks are equipped with speakers and microphones so we can communicate with each other.

"Let's move out," I said.

The team walked to the door. Patrick pushed the release button. The door hissed and opened exposing the rocky surface of the moon. John, the communications man, jumped out first; followed by Mick, Patrick, Austin and then Orlando. I was the last one out. We quickly got into formation and walked, more like jumped, toward the communications tower. We got to the door and pushed it open. All of us walked inside. I reached for the light switch and pushed it on. The room instantly illuminated with light. John took off his mask and began looking around. The room was large and had a computer system in the center. Surrounding the computer were endless buttons and a few screens. Further into the room was a staircase that led to the top of the antenna tower.

"Marshal," John called out to me. "There's something here you should see."

I walked over to John as he pointed toward the wall. Brown dried blood was smeared across like someone was using it as leverage to walk. I began following the trail. It led up to the tower staircase.

"Two line formation," I ordered. Orlando and Austin took point as Mick and Patrick got behind them. They slowly began to creep up the stairs when we heard it. A loud and sluggish moan blared above us.

"What the fuck was that?" Mick said not able to see what made the noise.

"It sounds like someone's in trouble," Orlando answered.

We heard steps beginning to descend from the staircase. And soon enough, as the light illuminated the body, we saw it. The image of the man still haunts me till this day. His skin was pale and green. It was missing part of its right cheek revealing teeth and jaw. The man's nose was broken and looked to have been smashed back into his face. Most of its hair was ripped out of its scalp. The monster continued walking down to us as we stared in shock.

"Fall back," I said.

The creature tripped over its feet and tumbled down the remaining steps. It landed face first on the ground making a sickening thud only a foot away from Orlando. We stared at it for a moment, pointing our weapons as it remained motionless. There were gashes on its arm where bone and muscle tissue disgorged out of.

"What is it?" Patrick asked.

"I don't know," I answered. None of us had ever seen anyone who looked like this and still was able to walk.

When I said that, the creature sprang to life. It wrapped its hands around Orlando's shin and dragged itself toward him. The beast sank its teeth into Orlando's calf ripping away chunks of clothes and flesh. He screamed in pain as Austin came to his aid. He pulled the creature from Orlando and shoved him away kicking it across the face. Orlando tried to shift weight from his bitten leg. He lost balance and fell back as blood gushed out of his wound. He continued to scream. We were all dumbfounded at what this cannibalistic person did. I began to shout orders.

"Patrick, take Orlando to the entrance and wrap something around his leg. Everyone else fall back, get away from this thing."

The creature began to rise to its feet. It chewed on the hunk of Orlando's flesh. Blood gushed out of its mouth and dripped onto the ground as it chewed. Patrick grabbed Orlando by his suit and dragged him to the door. The creature shambled toward us.

I raised my rifle and pulled the trigger. The bullet entered the beast's chest and exploded out of its back. A golf ball size hole appeared where the bullet traveled. It continued walking toward us.

"Fire," I said in shock. No one alive would be able to survive a shot through

98

the chest. Everyone around me raised their weapons and fired. Bullets began to rip through the creature's body; black substance poured out of the open wounds. It fell back and thrashed on the ground. Bullets ricocheted within the room, but luckily no one was struck.

"It's still alive," Austin said in terror as it got back to its feet. The bullet holes all over its body were oozing out black bile.

Mick turned the S-801 rifle scope on. He raised it up to his eyes as best as he could and fired a round through its skull. The impact caused the top of its scalp to rip open, exposing what was left of its black brain. Mick fired again, this time hitting it center forehead. Brain tissue splattered across the wall behind it. The creature fell to the ground smacking what was left of its head on the stairs railing.

Austin turned to tend to his older brother while the rest of us stood in alarm. I shook off my fright and walked toward Orlando. He had a rag tied a little above his knee.

"That's all I could find," Patrick said.

Orlando began to cough up the same black matter as the monster. He curled to his side and vomited. Bile spewed out from his mouth, nose and even his eyes.

"We need to get him back to the ship," I said.

Mick walked up behind me and said, "No,

we can't. It looks like that creature over there is infected with something. Orlando has it. He needs to stay here and we should get away from him before we get infected."

Austin was the first to say something, "We're not leaving my brother behind."

The more I thought about the situation, the more I realized that Mick was right. The creature was infected with something. I looked over to John who quickly put his mask back on. Orlando began to convulse on the ground. His skin was turning green and his face was covered in sores.

"Look at him," Mick said. "We need to get out of here."

"No, we're not leaving him," Austin answered.

I looked down at Orlando, he stopped moving. Austin was to busy arguing with Mick to realize what was going on. Orlando's eyes turned black as he stumbled to his feet.

Mick saw him rise and quickly took a few steps back. Austin had his back to him; he slowly turned to look at his brother.

"Orlando?" he said as it lunged for him. Orlando ripped Austin's mask off and bit into his face over his right eye. He sucked the eye out of his socket then chewed. Austin shrieked in pain as he pushed his brother back and covered his wound. Orlando lunged again for him biting into his chin. Mick raised his weapon to his eye and fired. The bullet traveled through Austin's head and exited into Orlando's skull. Both of them crashed to the ground on top of each other as blood and brain matter seeped out of the wounds.

"Sorry, sir," Mick said to me.

I didn't blame him, I actually believed his reasoning. Orlando was bitten and he turned. Austin was bitten and he would have turned. Destroying the brain was the only thing that brought down the first creature.

"No need to be sorry," I added. "You did what you had to." I did feel bad for my two fallen men. But I had seen a lot of death. "Listen up," I said to the remaining team. "We need to take their bodies back to the ship. If this is an infection, Zilith will need to study it. All of the communications equipment looks fine. I'm guessing that no one wanted to come in because that thing was here. After we take Orlando and Austin back to the ship we'll head for the resort."

"How are we going to take the bodies? I'm not touching them," Mick said.

I looked around and saw a roll of plastic wrap in the corner. I grabbed it and began wrapping the dead bodies.

"They look like mummies," Patrick said.

"No jokes, these men use to be our teammates," I said as I grabbed Orlando's body and flung him over my shoulders.

John stood by the door. He nodded and opened it. I walked through the door with him over my shoulder. Patrick and Mick carried Austin behind me. John held his

weapon up in case there was another creature lurking in the shadows.

We made it to the ship and put their
bodies in the cargo area underneath the
craft. John locked the doors and turned to
face us.

"Should we call this in?" John asked.

"No," I answered. I didn't want to call
anything in until I could confirm what
happened to the occupants at Moonlit Resort.

We headed north toward the hotel. From
our landing point we could see the structure about a mile away. We trekked with
worry and alarm plastered on our faces.

"I can't believe that Austin and Orlando are dead. What the hell was that
thing?" John said breaking the silence.

"I don't know," I admitted. "Mick might
be right when he said infection. Have you
ever read *War of the Worlds*? The Martians
thought they could come and take Earth
away from us. Despite everything humanity
threw at them, it was an infection that
ultimately killed off the alien invaders.
I think here, we are the aliens and the
moon is telling us to leave."

No one spoke after my comment. Maybe
they were trying to process what was happening here.

We finally reached the structure. The
three-story high hotel was built on a
large block of pavement. It was gray and
made out of mostly steel. A well-lit green
sign that flashed the words; *MOONLIT RE-
SORT was* positioned just above the double

doors.

The doors to the building were shut. I took point as I pushed open the first set of doors. Patrick was at the rear, he closed the doors behind him. A robotic voice welcomed us and let us in through the second set of doors. Oxygen began to blow into the room as the last set of doors opened. We held our weapons up as the automatic doors opened.

The lobby was completely decimated. Sofas were overturned. Broken glass and miscellaneous papers littered the ground. Splatters of blood and pieces of bone and meat were spewed all over the room. I slowly crept into the room. The front desk was to my right. Straight ahead was a large dinning room and to the left were two stair cases and the elevators.

"Hello?" I called out as the lights flickered.

There was no response.

"This is Space Marshal Collins, if anyone is there please respond."

Nothing.

We walked in a square shape formation. First we went through the dining room doors. The lights were off, I flipped the switch next to the door and the florescent lights blinked on. All of the tables and chairs were overturned. Some were broken. Dishes and expired food covered the ground.

"Hello?" I said again, this time a reply came. Several collected moans echoed in the room. Bodies appeared to stand out of nowhere. Before we could blink the room was filled with at least thirty infected, each of them walked toward the open door. They stared at us with vacant and hungry faces. Among the horde of adults, were a few children as well. They were fast.

"Fall back," I said. As we turned we saw more of them pouring in from the staircase.

Mick raised the gun up his eyes and said, "Marshal, orders?"

I didn't hesitate to yell, "Fire!"

Mick fired four shots into the crowd to bring down the monsters closest to us. John and Patrick began firing wild, un-aimed shots. Surprisingly, they managed to drop a few. We were being cornered by the creatures. Their eyes hungrily stared at us as they advanced; tripping over the creatures we dropped.

We fell back toward the front desk.

"I'm running low," Mick yelled. "We need to find a way out."

As he said that, music began to play from the loud speakers. It was Jazz, some-thing I hadn't heard in years. The crea-tures stopped moving and stared to the sky. A dumbfounded expression crossed their face. Some sounded like they were humming along with the music. We kept fir-ing, dropping as many near the door as we could.

"We're going to run through them and make it to the door," I said.

We managed to make a path and began heading for the door. The music stopped when we were half way there. The creatures stopped staring into the loud speaker and turned too look at us.

I was taking point, Mick was behind me, John and Patrick were close behind. The creatures reach out for them. One of them managed to grab hold of Patrick's uniform. He had a few grenades strapped to his belt. The creatures yanked on the belt trying to bring Patrick closer, pulling the pin off one of the grenades. I remember hearing him scream as they pushed him back and forth. A loud beep erupted. The horde pulled Patrick deeper toward the dining room. He screamed louder as they began tearing him apart. We kept moving toward the door when the grenade exploded. Bodies flew in all directions and the building shook. The blast caused me to slam up against the door.

I heard a beeping noise and the doors opened. I crawled through and looked behind me. I couldn't see anyone from my team. All I saw were a few hungry faces staring at me and small patches of fire as the steel doors closed.

Everything else was a blur. I do remember crawling all the way back to the ship as the building burned from the inside. Luckily, Patrick had everything ready for takeoff. All I had to do was set the auto-pilot and the craft would do the rest.

When I made it back to Earth, I was instantly quarantined and put into the cell I'm in now. I was interrogated and accused of killing everyone there. I'm sentenced

to be hanged until I am dead. They would-
n't listen when I told them what happened
at the Moonlit Resort, about the strange
lunar infection that killed everyone and
turned them into mindless walking corpses.
Deep down inside, I have a feeling that
the Zilith Corporation knew what was going
on and they needed someone to blame. That
someone is me.

There was one thing I didn't tell them.
When I got back to the ship and took my
space suit off, I had these strange
scratches on my right shoulder that quickly healed before I landed on Earth. Maybe
while I was making my escape one of them
scratched me. I'll never know what kind of
an effect it'll have on me when I'm dead.

Space Marshal Elroy Collins
January 3rd 2060

Author Note:

I love Christmas. I love it a little too much.
My wife, Mandy, calls me a Christmas Freak.
And I'm ok with that, mostly because it's
true. In 2010, I set out to edit my own
Christmas themed anthology entitled, *The Undead That Saved Christmas*. Best thing about
that anthology, other than I was the one who
put it together, is that net proceeds go to
help buy Christmas presents for foster kids. I
wrote *The Gingerbreads* for that anthology. Being a Christmas kid at heart, I had a great
time writing this story and packed it with a
lot of Christmas carnage.

The Gingerbreads

"Can you see what's going on outside?" Fred asked his wife, Ginger, as they stared outside through the living room window.

"Yeah it's a bit dark, but I can see five of them. They're standing on the sidewalk looking toward the front door," she replied, trying to be as quiet as possible.

"Well why can't I see them?"

"How should I know?" she said in an agitated voice. "Come over here and look."

Fred walked toward Ginger, carefully stepping around the fully lit Christmas tree and jumping onto wrapped presents. He leaped off a medium size gift into a clearing and continued to hustle toward Ginger. "Why do you have the blinds open so far?" he asked concerned, then continued, "close them a little or they'll see us."

"Oh hush Fred, I don't think they are infected. I think they are normals." Ginger said still looking out the window.

"Normals!" Fred gasped frightened. "They're even worse than the infected. Do you think they know what we are?"

"I don't think they do."

"Here, let me look." Fred jumped up to the window, and then stared outside through an opening in the blinds. "Yup,

they are normals," he said as his eyes
made of frosting blinked. "Let's just wait
and hope some infected come. Wait a second. The normals are starting to swing
back and forth."

Ginger jumped onto the window ledge and
stood next to Fred, their little hands
touched. The five normals lit candles and
began to sing.

"Ohhhhhhh, weeeeeee, wish you a Merry
Christmas, we wish you a Merry Christmas,
we wish you a Merry Christmas and a Happy
New Year."

"So that's what they're doing," Fred
stated out loud.

"What?" Ginger asked. "What are they
doing?"

"They are carolers."

"Well what do they want?"

"I'm not sure. I'm not as old as you
might think. I was only baked about a week
ago. It seems to me that since it is
Christmas Eve they want to come in because
we have food."

"We do?" Ginger asked.

"Well yeah, I mean, right now I'm baking another batch of us so we can have
some Christmas company." It finally dawned
on Fred. He understood why the carolers
came to their front door. They knew that
this house had Gingerbread residents, and
the normals were hungry. Fred hopped in
the air and backed away from the window.
"Run, hide!"

"But why?" Ginger asked confused. "We
don't have any food."

"Ginger my love," Fred replied, "we *are* the food!"

"Oh, dear!" Ginger exclaimed as she jumped off the window ledge.

Fred ran toward Ginger and grabbed hold of her hand.

"This is what we are going to do." Fred pointed up to the Christmas tree. "We're going to pretend we're ornaments. Just jump onto the tree and hold on!"

Fred let go of Ginger's hand and jumped as high as he could. He grabbed on to a branch and blended in with the rest of the tree ornaments. Ginger was close behind.

"Now stand still," he said, "here they come."

At that moment, the front door swung open and the five normals slowly walked through the door. Fred felt the tree shake; he knew Ginger was scared, but there was no way the normals would find them on the Christmas tree.

The Gingerbreads stayed in their hiding spot while the normals ransacked the little home. Fred and Ginger didn't have much. It was only a one bedroom house with a kitchen and a bathroom. The previous owners were taken away by the infected a little after they baked a batch of cookies with the special dough. Fred was the only cookie left in the batch before the infected stormed the little house. No one could explain why the dough was magical, but soon after the normals were taken, the little Gingerbread man moved. Fred was not the first Gingerbread to get up and walk.

This magical dough has been around for as long as the undead have.

After standing still for five minutes Fred smelled something foul. The oven was still on and their Gingerbread brothers and sisters were surely roasted by now. *Oh, what a terrible way to go,* Fred thought, *that's even worse than being eaten by a normal!*

A normal male quickly ran toward the kitchen. Fred couldn't see what they were doing, but he did hear the racket. They took the baking pan out of the oven and slammed it on the stove.

"Dinner time!" one of the normals yelled.

Fred heard the faint cries of his Gingerbread friends as they were devoured by the normals. The half-burned Gingerbread people wailed in pain one by one.

"No please don't!"

"Please, nooooooo!"

"I've never had a chance to live."

"I hope you burn your mouth you filthy normal!"

A tear made of vanilla frosting fell down Fred's face.

The five normals came back into the living room. They wiped their mouths and dusted the leftover crumbs off their clothes. One of them looked directly at the Christmas tree, directly at Fred and Ginger. That is when they heard it, the moans of an undead.

'*Oh thank heavens,*' Fred thought as he heard dragging footsteps coming closer to the open front door.

The normal male had forgotten all about the hiding Gingerbread cookies. The tables had turned. The caroling normals were no longer the hunters they were now the hunted. The undead don't like to eat Gingerbread people, but they sure do like themselves some normal's flesh. Gingerbread and the undead are not friends, but they are not enemies either.

Fred broke character so he could see the reaction of the normals that were now frantically searching their little home for weapons.

"I can't find anything," one of the normals said.

"Well what do you expect? Gingerbread people live here now. The only stuff you'll find is baking utensils. That's all they seem to do."

"What? Bake?"

"Yup, they love baking more cookies. Which is good for us, their cookies are always delicious."

"Both of you hush up," a stern female voice said. "The zombies are coming. We need to get ready to fight them off. Whose bright idea was it to carol sing anyway? I'm sure that's what brought them."

No one answered the voice. The moans and footsteps grew closer. Any second now the Gingerbread will see their saviors. Fred looked toward Ginger's hiding spot but she was gone. He nervously searched the area and called out her name. There was no response. He peered down and spotted Ginger already sitting on the edge of a present waiting for the show. Fred smiled and his love for Ginger renewed, he was very glad he made her first. Fred jumped off the tree and sat on the edge of a present next to his cookie love. It was almost show time.

"Look there's one!" said Ginger pointing at the first zombie that stumbled into the door.

"One of them is inside!" a normal yelled, while another asked, "Who left the door open!?"

Ginger and Fred giggled at the unprepared normals. One of the normals rushed out of the kitchen with a toaster in his hands. He raised his pathetic weapon and brought it crashing down on the zombie's head. It staggered back but didn't fall. The normal raised the toaster again, but the undead lashed out toward the man. It grabbed hold of him and quickly bit into his neck. Blood gushed out of his wound like a fountain, squirting the zombie's face with blood. The toaster fell out of his hands.

Another normal hurried out of the kitchen. She stared at the scene and yelled, "Frankie no!" She leaped onto the zombie's back who was still biting into the man's neck. She pried the zombie away from the normal she called Frankie. A large chunk of Frankie's neck tore loose as the infected was pulled away. Frankie fell to the floor holding his neck. Blood continued to gush out of his wound, which was now seeping through the cracks of his fingers.

The normal female pushed the zombie back and took a large knife out of her makeshift holster. She waited for the zombie to lunge and when it did, she forced the knife under its chin and through the zombies head. The blade slid easily into the creature's head, then stopped when the tip poked out of its scalp. She forced the knife out again and the infected fell to the ground. She ran for the door and closed it. Pounding erupted from outside the door.

The other three normals ran out of the kitchen.

"Thanks for the help!" the woman normal yelled as she pressed her body against the back of the door. She looked down toward Frankie, who was now motionless and lying in a pool of his own blood, and then continued, "Frankie's dead!"

* * *

"All right!" Ginger cheered, a little louder than she should have. "The infected got the one that saw us."

"Shhh," Fred replied. "We're not in the clear yet. There are still four of them."

"Poor Frankie," one of the normals said.

Two normals pressed up against the door alongside the woman with the large knife. A loud crash echoed through the house as one of the infected came stumbling through the window next to the Noble Fir Christmas tree. It rolled into the house knocking the tree over. Ornaments flew everywhere.

"Ahhhh!" the two Gingerbread yelled, as the Noble Fir came crashing down onto them. Fred managed to jump out of the way, but Ginger leaped toward the normals.

* * *

The infected that smashed its way through the window rose to its feet. Its eyes began to glow red.

The normal not holding the door yelled worriedly, "Its eyes are red! I've never seen any of them do that!"

"Don't be stupid Brad, the Christmas lights are reflecting off its eyes. Go take it out!" the woman with the sword like knife yelled.

More pounding erupted from the other side of the door. More infected were trying to get in.

* * *

Fred yelled as loud as his little Gingerbread voice could go. "Giinnngeerr!" But there was no reply. He couldn't see Ginger from where he was, somewhere inside the tree's branches and next to the presents. Fred grabbed hold of a tree branch and found his way to the middle of the tree. He ran as fast as his little legs could go to make it to the tree stump. He was in a clearing of the fallen branches and, from

his position, he could see the fight continuing between the normals and the infected.

* * *

The normal named Brad rushed toward the
infected. He had the large baking pan that
Fred used to bake more Gingerbread cookies
in his hands. He raised it up and brought
it down on the zombie's head. A loud smack
echoed in the room. He hit the undead
again and again until the infected was on
the ground. Brad jumped into the air and
came crashing down onto the zombie's head,
near its mouth. The zombie's eyes popped
out of their sockets and flew into the
air. Blood, goop and other unidentified
matter exploded out of the zombies head
like a party popper, spraying the normals
at the door with infected juice. The two
eyeballs arched in the air like a rainbow
and landed near the kitchen's entrance
with a smack. The eyes proceeded to roll
into the kitchen and out of sight.

"Brad, you freaking idiot!" one of the
normal yelled, "I'm not going to be able
to take a shower for a long time."

Brad didn't look down at the mess he
knew the zombie was in. If he did look,
then he would surely vomit the burnt Gingerbread cookies he ate. He searched
around the room for a sheet or something
to cover the body. More pounding came from
the door. The normals were not going to be
able to hold the door forever.

* * *

"Ggggiinnnnggeeerrrr!" Fred yelled from the tree stump. Again there was no answer. He began to worry for his little Gingerbread wife. *I need to find higher ground*, Fred thought. He had the option of running toward the couch on the other side of the living room. Without hesitation the little six inch tall Gingerbread man began running in that direction.

There was no need to worry about being seen. The normals were no longer interested in finding more Gingerbread cookies. They were more interested in survival.

Fred jumped and leaped through the overturned tree until he made it to the top. The sofa was only a few feet away, but from the point of view of a Gingerbread man – it looked like miles. He jumped off the tree and headed for the couch. Fred looked toward the panicking normals then glanced at the body of Frankie whose eyes have begun to flutter open.

* * *

"Stop looking around and help us hold the door closed," the woman with the large cook's knife yelled at Brad.

"Okay, Sandra," Brad replied as he walked toward the door.

None of the non-infected noticed that Frankie's eyes have opened, especially

Brad. He carefully stepped over Frankie's body not wanting to look down. Frankie grabbed a hold of Brad's exposed leg. He gasped and looked down to see Frankie snapping his jaw toward his calf.

"Look out!" someone yelled, a little too late. Frankie already had his teeth around Brad's leg. He howled in pain then tried to shake Frankie away. His jaw locked and sunk further into Brad's calf. Blood dripped out of the wound and flowed into Frankie's mouth.

Without a second thought Sandra jumped away from the door and ran toward Brad. She pulled the knife out of the makeshift holster and slashed across Brad's throat. Blood squirted out of the wound as a sorrow filled look washed over Brad's face.

Brad tried to force the word *why* out but fell to the ground before he could do so. Sandra took the knife and jammed it into the side of Frankie's skull. She pulled the knife out and brain matter oozed out of the hole.

* * *

Fred made it to the couch and climbed up the side. The little Gingerbread man was sweating vanilla frosting from all the running and jumping. He walked to the edge of the cushion and sat.

"Ginger where are you?" said Fred out loud to himself.

"I'm over here," a reply came from the other end of the couch.

"Ginger!" Fred yelled, as he stared into her cookie face. "I was so worried I had no idea where you were." Fred ran toward Ginger as he spoke.

"I'm fine silly," she said, "I ran over here because the tree was blocking my view. I wanted to see the action!"

That last comment frightened Fred, but he brushed the feeling away and gave Ginger a nice long hug. They held hands and sat on the edge of a cushion to watch the rest of the show.

* * *

"Damnit Sandra! What did you do that for?" a voice questioned.

"I had to!" she snapped back angry with herself. "It was my fault! I should have destroyed Frankie's brain when he was bitten."

Sandra hurried toward Brad who was laying face down on the floor. He was motionless and had been drained of his life essence. Sandra raised her knife in the air.

"We can't hold the door any long—" The same voice cried as the undead broke through.

Sandra lowered her knife and headed for the kitchen. The other two normals followed close behind.

The zombies poured into the living room like a flood. Some walked in through the door as others stumbled in through the broken window. The first few zombies instantly knelt in front of Frankie and Brad's bodies on the floor. The dead began feasting on their flesh as the next wave of undead headed to the kitchen in search of more prey.

* * *

"Aww," Ginger sighed, "they went into the kitchen, we can't see them anymore. Come on let's go after them."

Ginger stood and leaped off the couch then ran toward the kitchen.

"Wait!" Fred pleaded. "Don't! You're going to get trampled by the undead!"

Ginger ran into the horde of zombies nearly getting smashed to pieces by their feet. Fred lost sight of her as she made her way into the kitchen. *Why is she being so reckless?* Fred thought as he leaped off the couch after her.

"Ginger!" Fred yelled. He ran straight into the undead. There was no fear in his eyes. He had to save the woman he loved. Fred jumped and dodged the feet of the walking dead. Drops of blood fell from above, nearly splattering the little Gingerbread man with tainted juice. Fred ran as fast as he could and made his way through the kitchen entrance.

Fred made a funnel using his little hands and put them around his mouth then yelled, "Ginger!" He looked around trying to find her, but the entire room was completely filled with the infected.

"Up here!" a familiar voice shouted.

Fred looked up toward the kitchen table and there was Ginger. She sat on the edge of the table, staring out into the crowd of the undead. She looked down at Fred and waved.

Fred grabbed onto a table leg and began to climb up. He made it to the top and the two Gingerbread people reunited. Fred hugged Ginger as they both stared at the slaughter.

* * *

"There's no place to go," Sandra cried from behind their little barricade which consisted of a refrigerator lying on its side. "This isn't going to hold them forever!" She glanced to the floor and staring back at her were the zombie's missing eyes.

The two normal men tried to open the little window above the sink. They managed to get it open and one of them crawled out, only to be grabbed by the dead waiting on the other side. The man still inside the kitchen closed the window when he saw the hideous face of a living dead woman.

More zombies piled into the little kitchen. The normal man looked over to Sandra for orders, but she had already taken her life. He saw the handle of her knife lodged in the side of her head. Blood oozed out of her wound as she lay still on the floor.

The undead clawed over the barricade and grabbed hold of the man. He screamed in pain as the first undead bit into his cheek. The undead piled on top of the man causing him to fall back. The slaughter was over and the living dead had won.

* * *

"Wow, what a show," Ginger said enthusiastically. "What happens now?"

"Well," Fred answered, "they will finish eating the normals then scatter out of here like roaches to find more food."

"Cool." Ginger added, "So they don't eat us correct?"

"No," Fred answered.

"Can they talk?"

"I don't know to tell you the truth." Fred responded. He turned to face Ginger only to see her jump off the table.

"Hey zombies!" Ginger yelled, "Hello? I'm talking to you."

Fred ran to the edge and peered down toward Ginger.

"Ginger! Stop that! Get back up here and leave them alone!"

Ginger ignored Fred's plea. A zombie peeked down at the little cookie making the noise. He knelt down to examine it. Fred watched in horror as the undead lifted Ginger off the ground. The zombie then licked Ginger from head to toe, its saliva getting into her mouth and any other openings.

"Ginger!" Fred yelled.

The zombie finished licking Ginger, and then placed her next to Fred. It turned and started walking out of the kitchen. All of the zombies followed. Fred suspected that they had run out of food.

Ginger lay motionless on the table. Fred knelt before her and began to weep. He knew that Ginger was dead. The infection got inside of her and now she was dead. Fred, however, didn't know how the zombie infection would affect a Gingerbread person if it did at all. He watched Ginger as the zombies cleared out of the house, leaving skeletons of the normals scattered around their home. Fred heard the door slam shut, then Ginger's frosting eyes opened.

"Ginger!" Fred yelled, "Are you alright my dear?"

"Yes," she replied, "I'm fine, but I must infect the normals."

"Eh?" Fred questioned. "What are you talking about?"

"Something inside of me is saying that I must infect the other normals. Where are they, Fred?"

"I ... I don't know," Fred answered in a frightened voice.

There was a new look to Ginger, something almost sinister. There was a calmness to her voice also, as if she wasn't the same cookie she once was.

"What do you know about this Santa Claus?" the undead Gingerbread cookie asked.

"Um ... not much. I know that he comes

to all the good kid's homes to give them presents. He loves eating cookies and drinking milk."

"And what time does Santa Claus come?"

"Overnight, I guess."

"Thank you, Fred," Ginger said as she paced on the kitchen table.

Fred turned around, not wanting to look at the Gingerbread cookie who once was his loving wife. She was now an infected cookie and he wanted nothing to do with her. He had to slay her. He could always make himself a new companion. When the thought crossed his mind, he heard fast approaching footsteps.

Fred spun around only to see Ginger charging toward him. She knocked the little Gingerbread man off the table with a force Fred didn't know she had. Fred flew into the air and landed on the ground ten feet away. His neck broke when he fell, sending his head skidding a few feet away from his body.

* * *

"Ho, Ho, oh my," a jolly old voice said. "It looks like there have been some naughty zombies here. Oh, how I hate those things," Santa grumbled. The Big Guy dressed in red walked around the living room and examined the skeletons on the floor. "Ah, Brad and Frankie, you were two good boys when you were children. I am so sorry. No one deserves to be eaten."

Santa noticed a pleasing aroma coming from the kitchen. He instantly forgot about the bones on the floor and made his way into the kitchen. The smell of freshly baked Gingerbread cookies was coming from somewhere. Saint Nick glanced toward the table and there was a female Gingerbread cookie lying next to a note. He grabbed the note and read it aloud.

"Santa, please enjoy this special Gingerbread cookie, then spread your holiday cheer." He smiled and picked up the Gingerbread cookie. He turned the cookie around and written in frosting was the name, Ginger.

"Thank you, Ginger," he said, and then ate the cookie. "That was the best Gingerbread cookie I've ever had."

Santa turned and headed back to the chimney. "Oh, something is making my belly shake like a bowl full of jelly," Santa snarled as he made his way back up the chimney. He knew something was wrong, but didn't know what, until he sat in his sleigh and closed his eyes. A tiny little voice inside of him began to speak.

"Thank you for eating me, Santa. I have succeeded in spreading the zombie infection." Santa's eyes widened, he realized that he was now becoming a zombie himself. The sleigh took off into the cold December night to the next house where Santa will spread his new holiday cheer.

**RADIO
DEAD**

Author Note:

In 2011, KnightWatch Press took a chance on my
novella, *Dement*, and published it. At the time
of this author note, it has not been released.
Once people begin to read it, they might notice something between this story and a few
others with, *Dement*. Let me clarify. When I
wrote, *Dement*, I had an idea. I wanted to have
a main story and have other stories spin off
from the original story. For example, in *Dement,* the main character, Mark, turns the radio on and The Manny Mayhem Morning Show is
on. *Radio Dead* was created as a spin off from
that story. Once the full version of *Dement* is
released and people read my short stories, I
hope I did a well enough job to where the
readers can start connecting the dots.

Radio Dead

The Manny Mayhem Morning Show waited patiently in the broadcasting studio for their producer. It was 5:00 a.m. and the crew was set to go on the air in half an hour. While they waited, the cast reviewed their notes and the list of radio bits they would perform.

Manny Mayhem stared intently at his laptop computer screen. He sat on the edge of a long table, where they also record their radio show. Two members of the cast were on both sides of the table, sitting across from each other. The producer would sit on the other edge of the table but he was running late.

"Damn!" Manny Mayhem said, breaking the silence. "This shit is everywhere."

The other four people in the room looked up from their notes and glanced toward Manny.

"What is it?" Manny heard someone say. He was too far into his daze that he could not comprehend who asked the question.

"This virus, or infection, or whatever the fuck it is." Manny shook his head as he leaned back on his rolling chair. He continued to stare at the computer display.

The doors that led into the small studio swung open as Petite Pete stormed in. The small thirty-two-year-old man held his brown briefcase under his right armpit, and with his left hand he wiped away sweat from his forehead. Pete walked toward his empty chair and put his briefcase onto the table. With one swift movement he opened the case, brought out his laptop and placed it in front of him.

"You're late," Manny said in a playful tone, then continued, "next time I'm going to have your thumbs." He pointed to himself with his thumbs as the cast laughed. The hair from his goatee reached his nostrils as he smiled.

Everyone in the room knew that Pete didn't have thumbs. They constantly gave him grief for it, but Pete was always in high spirits—except for today. He wasn't having any of it.

"Shut up, Manuel. I'm in no mood for your shit today," Pete said, setting up his laptop.

Manny's smile grew bigger now that he got a rise out of Pete. "Aww, what's the matter? Did someone not get their morning lay?" Manny joked. The two females in the room giggled.

"Manny stop," Pete said sternly, "I've got a headache, I'm sweating like a pig and my body aches. I just want to get this day over with and go home."

"All right, all right," Manny uttered as he lifted his arms in defeat.

The cast of the Manny Mayhem Morning Show continued to prepare for the broadcast. Everyone was quiet and concentrating on the notes for the day. Manny continued to read the news headlines off his laptop screen. He e-mailed the top headlines to the news girl.

An alarm began to sound, waking the crew out of their daze. There was five minutes before they were live on air. Manny Mayhem began flipping through the music files in his laptop. He searched for a song to bring them in. When he found the song, Manny clicked the play button. Petite Pete signaled the crew to put their headphones on. Everyone did, they also adjusted the microphones in front of them.

Creep by Radiohead blasted through their headphones. Petite Pete motioned toward Manny Mayhem to adjust the volumes, but he didn't listen. The song continued to play as loud as ever.

The song began fading out as the red 'On Air' sign lit up over their heads.

"Yeah! I love that song," Manny Mayhem said into the microphone. His voice changed from his speaking voice to his deep radio tone. "Welcome to the Manny Mayhem Morning Show. I am your manic host Manny Mayhem and all these guys and gals sitting next to me are my crew. As always I'm accompanied by our five foot nothing, little kid of a producer, Petite Pete. He looks a bit under the weather today, so if any of you *lovely* ladies listening wanna bring him some chicken noodle soup, we won't stop ya."

"I'm alright, Manny, there is no need," Pete chimed into the microphone.

Manny looked up toward Pete in surprise.

"Interrupt me again and I'll take your big toes too," Manny said jokingly, then continued, "now where was I?" Manny glanced to his left. "Ah yes, here to my left is the blond haired beauty, your dream girl and mine, our hot ass news girl, Reverse Cowgirl Kelly. Sitting next to her is the biggest man I've ever seen, Happy Pat, our sound effects man. Happy Pat why don't you show the listeners what you do."

Pat stared into his laptop, searching for a sound bite. *"Why do I got to be married to a crack-head?"* The sound bite echoed in their headphones, as someone chuckled into the microphone.

"All right, that made no sense but thank you, Happy Pat, now I know why I hired you." Manny now glanced to his right and faced the other crew members. "Sitting across from him rocking a white headband is our sports girl, that's right I said sports girl, Zoe. Might I say you look very good in that headband? And finally the closest to me on the right is the strangest, Mohawk wearing youngster I've ever met. He's our stunt boy, Babylon.

"Well, that's all of us," Manny glanced to his laptop, but continued talking into the microphone. "We have a great show for you guys this morning and we have lots to report. Cowgirl, what are the main headlines for today?"

"Residents from the little town of Bluebird County are advised to stay indoors. There are small groups of people that have been seen attacking anyone on the streets. The attacks consist of biting and scratching. The authorities are looking into this matter."

"Thanks, Cowgirl," Manny said. "Now do you wanna go to the back room?"

Cowgirl laughed, "Yeah right Manny, over my dead body."

Manny ignored the reply, and continued, "Where is Bluebird County anyway?"

"It's the next town over," Pete answered, "Don't let the name fool you. It's not really a county. That's just the name of the town."

"Thanks for clearing that up, Pete." Manny glanced down at his laptop. "Well, I don't think we have anything to worry about. We're safe in this building.

"If anyone is listening in Bluebird County, give us a call. None of the interns showed up today so Zoe is on phone screening. Let us know what's going on."

Pete began coughing in a violent rage into the microphone. Manny quickly shut off Pete's mic and asked, "Are you alright, buddy?"

Pete continued to cough.

"We are going to take a little break here so we can get Pete some water."

Manny made the arrangements and went to a commercial. All of the crew members took a step back as Pete continued to cough. Manny slowly walked toward Pete and gave him his water bottle. Pete took the offering and chugged down its contents.

"Maybe you should go home, Pete," Manny suggested.

"No, I'll be fine, I just needed some water," Pete replied.

Babylon edged over by a window that looked down to the parking lot. "Hey Manny, did you know we're the only ones here?"

"What?" Manny walked toward the window and looked outside. The only cars in the parking lot were from the six individuals in the room.

"Where is everyone?" Manny asked, then continued, "Pete did you see anyone on your way up?"

"No," came the faint reply. "I never really see anyone this early in the morning."

"You were the first one here Manny, did you see anyone?" Cowgirl asked.

"Now that I think about it no, I didn't." Manny stared in a trance, trying to remember his morning. "I came into the studio and everything was on auto pilot. There were songs being played so I thought the overnight guy set them and took off. It's not unusual so I guess I didn't think anything of it."

Manny heard the wrap-up signal. The commercials were coming to an end. He hurried back to the table and put on his headphones. Everyone else followed.

"And we're back. We gave Pete some water and it looks like he's going to make it. So, some strange stuff is going on outside. Zoe, do we have any calls yet?"

"Yeah," she replied, "the phones just started lighting up."

"Great, you don't have to screen them. I'll take a chance and answer the calls on air."

Manny pushed the button for line one.

"Hey caller, this is Manny Mayhem and you're on the air. Can you tell us what's going on out there? Just please don't curse."

"Hey Mayhem. Yeah there's some crazy stuff going on. I'm in my house and there are figures outside. I don't know what they want, but they're just there. I heard the news reports about a virus or something making people crazy. It's spreading really fast and I don't know what to do."

"Interesting, well the only advice I can tell ya is to stay inside and out of sight," Manny said to the caller. "Alright moving on, what does someone else have to say?"

Manny pushed line two.

"Hey caller, you're on the air."

"Manny, they are zombies man," the caller whispered.

"Huh? What do you mean?"

"The people outside, they're zombies."

"Like the flesh eating kind in movies?"

"Yeah man, zombies. I saw a group of them eating someone."

"How do you know this caller?"

"Manny, get out of your bubble, this has been going on here for a day or so. Don't listen to the news reports; it's far worse than what people are saying."

"Manny, we should go on to another caller. This guy's a loony," Pete interrupted.

Happy Pat played a sound effect referencing the strange caller as crazy.

"No hold on," Manny said, "I don't think this is a crazy call. Keep going caller."

"Thanks, Manny. I'm just looking out for my favorite radio show."

"No, thank you man, what else do you know? How can you tell they are zombies?"

"Well, I live in the heart of Bluebird County. My name is Joe and I'm a cameraman for the KBD news. Last night, we did a broadcast about the dead rising. My boss, Jason, was all excited about it. Even though people were dying, he wanted the ratings. We all thought the broadcast would reach a world wide audience, but by the time we reported it, most of the town was taken over. This is what I know, it's a virus that causes the recently dead to come back to life. They want to eat human flesh. If you get bitten or scratched you get infected. How fast you turn depends on where you were bitten. The further away from the brain the slower it takes. One good thing is that the zombies, undead, whatever, are very slow so you can easily out run them. The only way to stop them is by destroying the brain."

"That's fascinating stuff, Joe. Where are you holding up man?"

"I'm in an apartment building. The military is flying overhead yelling something over the intercom. I think they're saying to stay calm and stay indoors. I don't even live here, but I'm not going back outside, unless I have too."

"All right Joe, we gotta move on to another caller. Thanks a lot for calling in. Be safe man."

Manny pushed the button for line three. "Caller, what can you add to the subject?"

"Manny," a very soft and scared voice said. "It's true. I was listening on hold to the Joe caller and it's true. My husband died from a bite a few minutes ago. Not too long after his eyes reopened. I'm inside the bathroom and he's right outside the door. He's up and walking, I'm trying to be quiet because I know what will happen if he finds me. The radio is turned up all the way to drown out any noise I make in here."

A banging noise erupted from the phone call.
"He heard me," the caller said with terror in her voice, "I already tried calling the police but the lines were busy. I can't hold the door much longer. My husband was supposed to fix the door knob, but never did." She began to cry over the phone, then let out a scream. "He's here, stay back, Jim, stay baaaaack!" A moan echoed through the phone's speaker.

Manny quickly ended the call. Everyone was shocked at what they had just heard. The radio was completely silent for the first time.

"There's some real crazy stuff happen-

ing out there right now. Is this the apocalypse? I don't know but the dead have begun to rise. We are going to take a commercial break so we can figure out what to
make of this news. We'll be back."

The staff stared at each other. Pete
began to sweat again and then fell into
another coughing rage. Manny walked toward
the window to get another look at the
parking lot. It was almost 6:30 a.m. and
the sun was starting to poke out from the
mountains. The morning show was located
three stories high so Manny had a good
bird's eye view.

Manny stared out of the window. There
were no new cars in the parking lot, but
there were many human figures. His stare
finally focused on one. It was a woman
with long, dark hair. She slowly walked
away from the radio station. Her gray
skinned body bumped into one of the parked
cars but did not walk around. She continued to try and walk straight through the
vehicle. More of them that were on the
street began walking toward the radio station. They walked past the woman Manny was
examining. She turned around and followed
the horde as they walked toward the radio
station entrance.

They had lifeless stares on their
faces. Their eyes were cloudy and in an
instant they began to glow a faint red.
Manny snapped out of it when he noticed
they were coming toward the radio station.
He darted out of the room and ran down the
stairs to reach the doors before the dead

did.

After taking the last step down he heard them. The moans of the living dead echoed in his ears. The dead were already inside the first floor. He quietly made it back to the second floor and locked the door that led to the staircase from the inside. He continued to walk up the stairs to the third floor and locked that door.

He walked back into the room where the cast was huddled over their laptops looking for any information. In the heat of the moment, a thought occurred to Manny. He was not scared, but knowing that the dead were rising and there was no escaping made him realize he only had a short amount of time to live, therefore, he was going to make the most out of it.

"Listen up! I don't know if you guys have seen outside, but there's a shit load of them. They are in the lobby downstairs as well. We are trapped." Manny grinned maliciously. "This has turned into one great fucking show!"

Manny ran back to his chair and sat down. He put the microphone in front of him and began talking.

"All right everyone that's still alive and tuning in. We got ourselves a dilemma here at the radio station. All of the callers were 100% correct. I just ran into a few of the freaks. They made their way into the building and we're trapped. So how about we make the best of this situation and ..."

The power in the radio station suddenly went out. Everyone began to panic except for Manny; he was more pissed than anything.

"Ahh, great!" Manny said. "How am I supposed to conduct a radio show without power?"

"The power generators should come on any second now Manny," Pete said very faintly. "I'm not feeling well I'm going to go to the restroom." Before anyone could respond to him he was out the door with his briefcase. Pete shambled down the hall and entered the nearest restroom. He walked into a stall and began writing on a sheet of paper he took out of his briefcase.

Guys,

I was bitten yesterday by one of those things. I'm not feeling well and I'm sure it's from the virus. I don't want to become one of them and hurt any of you. This is probably the best thing for all of us. If you speak to my wife tell her I went down fighting.

Pete

Pete taped the note on the outside of the restroom door and came back into the stall closing the door behind him. He looked in his briefcase and found his 9mm Beretta handgun. Pete always carried his weapon for protection, but today he needed to protect himself from the beast growing inside of him. It took months, but Pete learned how to shoot a gun without thumbs. He placed the firearm under his chin; tears ran down his face as he pulled the trigger.

Blood, brain tissue and pieces of shattered skull spewed all over the bathroom stall. The top of his head was blown out by the force of the bullet. Pete's body instantly went limp.

The crew heard the blast and Babylon went to investigate. He walked into the bathroom and a terrible odor hit his nose. He walked to the stall where Pete took his life. The sight of Pete's half blown off head instantly made Babylon vomit. He let the door close and slowly walked out of the bathroom.

Babylon made his way back to the staff and reported what he saw. Everyone sat in silence.

"Even though we are down one man, the show must go on," Manny said with a devilish grin. The stress of losing his friend and being trapped took its toll on Manny. The power flickered back on and Manny quickly began setting up to broadcast again.

The whole cast followed Manny as he slowly went mad. They were trapped as well. The Manny Mayhem Show never mentioned Pete for the rest of the broadcast. They talked to the callers and signed off at their usual time.

The next morning the crew broadcast

their show and again the morning after that. Each day the show continued, the crew became more unstable. They began having radio bits involving zombies. Everything seemed safe but the stress overcame Zoe and Happy Pat.

One morning Manny woke up on his usual chair. He looked up where Zoe and Happy Pat slept, but they were gone. There was no note, no explanation for their leaving, they were just gone.

For some time the remaining crew did not broadcast a show. No one was listening anyway. They survived in the radio station eating anything they could find. The crowd of undead outside grew larger every day. None of them knew how much longer they could take being stuck in there. The smell in the room was unpleasant. None of them had been able to shower since the mess started.

Manny decided that the remaining crew would have one final show. Something that would give them a wonderful send off and then they would attempt to leave the radio station. Manny began planning the greatest show of his life. Manny had set the date for the following morning. Everyone lost track of time so there was no knowing when they last broadcasted.

Babylon was in charge of rounding up a zombie and bringing it into the room. It didn't go as planned. Babylon went to the lobby and tried to tie one up but was quickly overrun in seconds. The poor kid never had a chance.

Manny and Cowgirl were concerned when
Babylon never made it back. They walked
out of the room and headed toward the
stairs. The door swung open and a horde of
undead forced their way through. The one
in front was a zombified version of Babylon. Manny turned and began running toward
the station room. Cowgirl tripped over her
feet as she tried to get away. Manny
didn't notice until Cowgirl screamed out
in pain.

Babylon was on top of her legs. He had
been biting into her calf. Blood gushed
out of Cowgirl's leg when Babylon bit into
an artery. Manny hurried back to help Cowgirl, she outstretched her arm as Manny
grabbed it and yanked her away from the
advancing crowd. He lifted her in the air
and carried her back to the station room
leaving a line of blood on the floor. The
undead followed closely behind.

Manny closed the door and locked it behind him. He knew soon he would be alone.
Cowgirl was infected and would slowly turn
into a Freak. He didn't want to be alone;
Manny found a roll of duct tape and bonded
Cowgirl to the table. She was already
turning. Her large breast heaved up and
down instantly arousing him. Manny had not
been thinking clearly for the past few
weeks. The stress combined with the sorrow
he felt took over completely. The lovable
radio jockey was no longer there. He was
replaced by a sick and twisted individual.
He stared at Cowgirl as she took her last
breaths. This was the chance he had been

waiting for. It was the end of the world and he was going out with a bang.

Cowgirl's body lay limp as he undressed her. When he finished taking off her panties, Cowgirls eyes reopened. She began thrashing trying to loosen her bonds. She was strapped to the broadcasting table and Manny was lying on top of her. He quickly took off his pants and began to rub his penis. He spread Cowgirl's legs as best as he could and slid himself in. It had been a long time since Manny had sex so it didn't take long for him to climax.

The bonds on Cowgirl loosened and with a final jerk, she broke through the tape. As Manny climaxed Cowgirl reached for his shoulder with her mouth and closed her jaw. The pain mixed with the climax gave Manny the best orgasm of his life.

Cowgirl continued to bite until she ripped a chunk of Manny's shoulder. He held her down with his arm as blood poured out of the wound. In agony, Manny slid his penis out of the zombie and cleaned it with his shirt. He continued to use the shirt to press against the wound on his shoulder.

Manny wasn't going to wait a full day to get his final broadcast out. The day was ruined as soon as it started. He carefully let Cowgirl Kelly get to her feet and tied her naked body to the chair next to him. Manny set everything up to start a broadcast. He brought a microphone up to his mouth and began.

"All right everyone who's still listening, we haven't had a caller in a long time, mostly because we took some time off of the airways. I got some good news and some bad news to report. The good news is that I finally fucked Reverse Cowgirl Kelly and man what a lay. The bad news is our producer, Petite Pete, blew his brains out after he started showing signs of the infection. His body is in a bathroom stall. We don't use that shitter anymore. Babylon painted RIP on the door. Speaking of Babylon, that stunt boy has seen his last day. A freak got him while he was trying to round one up for our 'What's a Zombie Thinking?' bit. I'm not sure where everyone else ran off to. The only ones here are myself, Manny Mayhem and the lovely Reverse Cowgirl Kelly. Why don't you say hello to the listeners?"

Cowgirl stared at the microphone as if she knew what to do. She slowly put her mouth to it and let out a moan.

"Now, now," Manny continued, "before everyone starts asking questions, we had sex *after* she turned. Boy was she a biter. She bit me on the shoulder. Man she was rough. She even nibbled a piece of my prick off. Just playing, but remember how I always tried to get her to sleep with me? She always said over my dead body. Well ... it was wonderful. That's all I have to say about that. This is my final broadcast and I am signing off forever. I have no regrets and I'd do everything all over again if I could. The Freaks or as Cowgirl called them, Cupids, are banging on the door. Oh and while we were gone I found out why she decided to call them Cupids. It was because ..."

The door broke open as the Freaks stormed into the room. "Well never mind, they are in the room and I don't have much time but this is Manny Mayhem signing ..."

Manny didn't get to finish his normal sign off. The Freaks got to him and pulled him away from the microphone. He screamed as six different mouths bit down on his flesh. After a moment he stopped fighting. Blood squirted out of every wound on his body. They proceeded to rip his stomach open revealing all of his intestines. Hands reached inside his body and yanked out any piece possible. The feasting lasted fifteen minutes.

By the time the freaks were done with Manny Mayhem he was nothing more than a skeleton from the neck down. His head was still intact, none of the Freaks paid attention to his head. A few moments after death, Manny's eyes reopened and began looking around the room. As he tried to move, his head detached from his body and rolled under the table where his mind will rest eternally.

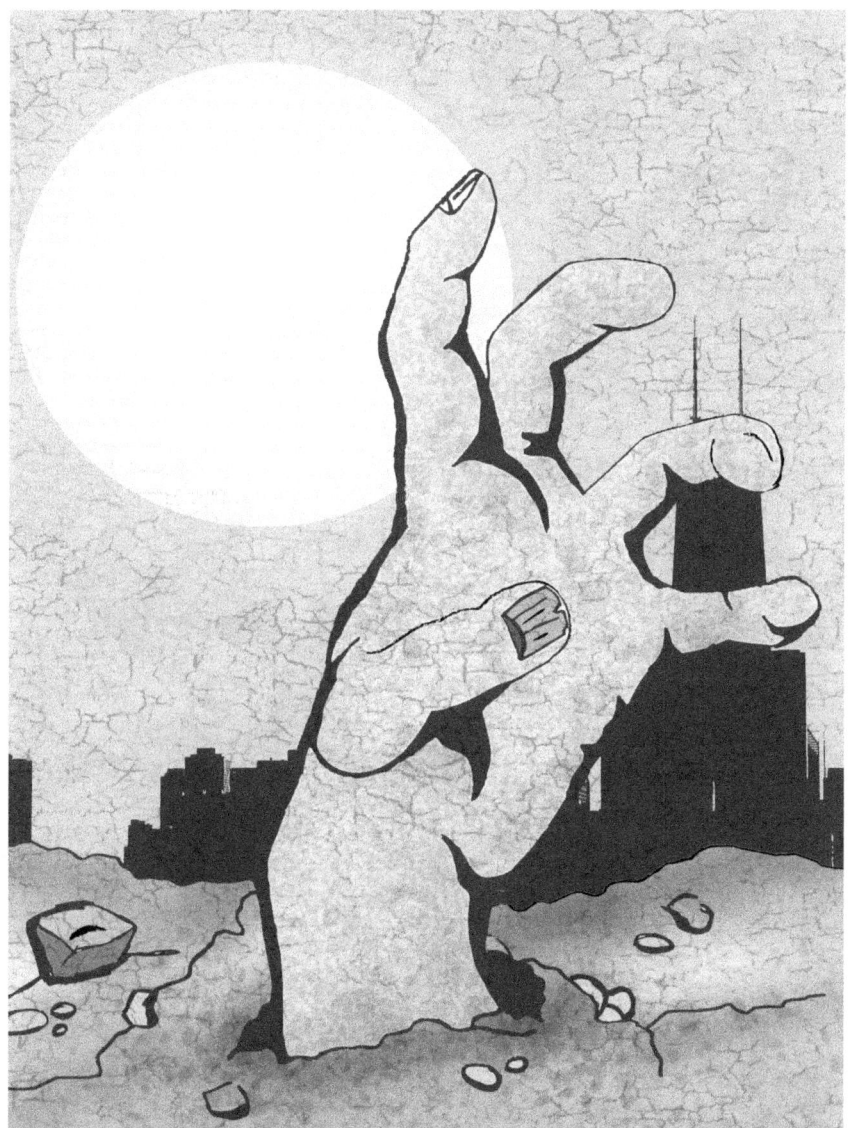

DEAD of OLD

Author Note:

Dead of Old was my first accepted story to an anthology, but not my first published. This story appeared in the anthology, *Eye Witness: Zombie*. I don't want to get into details, but I had my story pulled from that anthology. Remember in my previous author note, I mentioned about my stories linking with each other? *Dead of Old*, also links back to *Dement* and *Radio Dead*. I did this in such a way where each story works solo, meaning that you don't have to read *Dement* to understand *Radio Dead* and vice versa. The links are subtle to where the reader won't notice them, unless they've read my other stories.

Dead of Old

I'm sitting inside my cubicle watching old videos on *YouTube*. I can't believe it's been a year since the dead walked the earth. What a horrific time in our lives that was for every survivor. I myself still have dreams about the despicable acts I committed to stay alive. I can guarantee that no one who lived through the outbreak will ever be the same. Gone are the days when people helped each other or were at least friendly. Well, I shouldn't say that. Society is starting to come together again but very slowly.

I'm watching a video uploaded by someone with the username *MarkB_DementKilla*. According to his bio and video description, he was a lone survivor who holed up on the roof of a pawnshop for the first three months of the outbreak. After that, he was holed up in a place a few blocks away from my house. It looks like the video was recorded at his home.

In the first part of the video, he runs around aimlessly. Nothing really happens until the next part when the front door of his home swings open and the undead walk in. Gunshots erupt as blood spews from the zombies' heads. Each of them fall and another group of five zombies comes surging in.

The living dead don't usually move

fast; they shamble and step very slowly. But once one of them is close to a living person, it jumps to life. Think of it like a Jack in the Box; you turn the crank until the Jack springs out. With the undead, you're the crank, and once you're close enough, they spring to get you.

By now, MarkB_DementKilla has run out of rounds, so he wields a *Katana* blade. I can see why he survived. Mark is very calm and shows no fear as he thrusts the Samurai sword and swings without hesitation, decapitating zombies with every blow. I can only imagine how the blade's handle feels as it slices through flesh and bone. Blood sprays out from a flying head and mists on the camera lens. The clip continues to play, but all I can see is blood. After thirty more seconds of MarkB's grunts everything goes quiet. The camera is picked up and the blood is wiped away.

MarkB_DementKilla's weary, but his pleased face is displayed on the screen, and says, "Now that is how you kill some fucking dements."

The screen turns black, and the *YouTube* video recommendation tabs appear. I scroll through the recommendations and begin to realize how much life has changed since the outbreak.

It's been about seven months since I last saw an infected person. Long enough that I don't expect to see them anymore. The military took the remaining dead to a research facility where they try to learn as much from them as possible. It's pretty secure. Bluebird County residents are allowed to visit the facility, but no one really does. The town fought the government until they were granted minimal clearance to enter the facility. Now that we got it, no one wants to go near it. I guess we are all trying to forget the undead and what happened.

I've been drinking soda all morning. This can's almost empty so I take the last drink and toss it into the recycle bin under my desk.

I step out of my cubicle and take a quick look around. My co-workers are all staring at their computers typing away. I'm not sure if they're really working or just pretending, but I don't care; I just have to piss. I push my rolling chair back and walk down the little hallway that leads to the only exit out of this room.

I continue down the hall that leads to the HR department. Empty offices line up on my right, and further down the hall to my left are more cubicles. Most of the HR employees are glued to their computers just like the staff in my department. Brenda is the only one who acknowledges me as I walk down the hall.

"Hey Joe," she says.

"Hey Brenda," I reply without stopping. I really have to piss. I just want to make it to the restroom.

I make a right at the end of the hall and push open the blue door that leads into the break room. The aroma of fresh popcorn greets my nose. I immediately turn to the left and the door to the ladies' restroom is in sight, and the men's room awaits just a little further down. I push the door open. Thankfully, there is no one there.

I walk to a urinal and do my business.

On my return trip past HR, I pause. Out of the corner of my eye, I see something unsettling, a gray figure shuffling around outside. I turn to face the building's entrance. The glass door in front of the secretary's desk reveals just the sight I never thought to see again.

It is one of the undead, a male, walking up the pathway leading to the door. Behind him are another dozen. I freeze and continue to stare into his face as he shambles his way to the entrance. It doesn't appear as if he can see me. If he did, I would hear that terrifying moan.

He glances in my direction and gives me a lifeless stare. He is studying me, trying to determine if I'm friend or food. His lips twitch. When he realizes what I am, a moan erupts. It is the only signal I need. I sprint back up the hall, ignoring the questions from the HR folks as to why I'm running. The living dead have shambled into my life once again.

Forget everyone else. They can get eaten; I'm only looking out for myself, I think as I reach the door that leads back into my department. I brace my shoulders and crash through the push-handle door. The hinges creak and pop, and everyone in the office gasps.

Jamie, the lady closest to the door, says, "What's the matter?" I don't even answer her. My mind is somewhere else. I think about calling the police to report them, but if there are this many in one place, I'm sure they already know.

I sit back down in my chair and clutch my black mouse. I open a web browser, and the MSN news site is the first page I see. Big red letters cover almost half the page.

U.S. military has confirmed 100 infected have escaped from the Bluebird County Research Facility

"Fuck!" I say out loud. Everyone who wasn't looking at me before is sure looking now.

"What is it?" asks Carl, the large middle-aged man who sits to my right. Out of all of us, no one is as crazy as Carl. He decapitated his whole family after they turned. He said he did it with no remorse or feeling, but I don't believe that. Carl is either the most heartless person in the world or the biggest liar in the world. Either one is equally bad. No one in the office likes talking to Carl, but he's a good worker and he knows how to survive.

I stand up and get everyone's attention. "Look ... I just saw about a dozen infected outside. The one in front was at the door, and I'm sure he's trying to get inside by now." I motion to my computer screen. "It's on MSN. A hundred of them escaped from the research facility."

Panic and desperation claim every face. I don't know what everyone is so worried about. We've dealt with the undead before. The military did a great job containing all the infected, but that took months. Most people suffered the tragedy of having to kill at least one infected. The folks who had to kill one of their own family members had it the worst.

The door flies open again as the five employees from HR come rushing into our office, screaming hysterically. Brenda wails that a zombie just smashed the front door. Someone from HR calls me a jerk and threatens to report me for not alerting them of the infected outside. To whom I don't know, but I shrug the comment off. Typical HR attitude.

"Does anyone have any weapons?" I ask over the yelling.

Dave yells back, "I have a tire iron." He's the safety instructor. I guess he planned on using it for a demonstration.

I walk into his office and take the tire iron. Carl has already moved some filing cabinets and is pushing them toward the door.

"Hold on," I say as I grip the iron tight, "let me go out there and I'll take care of the one that got in."

The room becomes quiet as I pull the door open. I've only taken a few steps down the hall when I spot the infected male to my left. He sees me and lets out a moan. This is a fresh corpse, probably turned not long ago by one of the escapees. Unlike all the others I've seen, this one is sanitary. There is no blood on him, and his clothes look fresh. The only way I know he is infected is the moaning. And the eyes. Only the infected have red eyes that seem to glow when they notice food.

The undead are clumsy. They don't care if there's an object between you and them. Instead of walking around it, they'll try to go through it.

He walks toward me and bumps into a desk. I take advantage of his confusion and run at him, swinging the tire iron and crushing a small portion of his skull. The zombie tips over a chair as he falls backwards. He lies on the ground face up with the right side of his head split open. Blood gushes out of his wound.

I walk over to his body, his red eyes following me as I get closer. It doesn't look like he's able to move. I stand over his body and put the pointed end of the tire iron on his forehead. I slowly push down. The point enters his head swiftly, and I feel it puncture what's left of his skull as it passes through the brain.

No matter how many zombies you kill, the feeling of disgust never goes away. I wiggle the tire iron around to make sure I destroy as much of the brain as possible. You can never be too careful with the undead. When I finally pull my makeshift weapon out of his head, a long strain of brain matter follows behind.

I hold back my vomit. If it weren't the

only weapon we have, I would have just left it there. Instead, I grab a few Kleenex from a nearby desk and clean the mess off the tire iron, careful not to touch the blood with my bare hand. Even though they say you can't get infected from touching the blood, I don't want to take any chances.

Over the past few months the research facility has learned a lot from the undead. The biggest breakthrough as of late is that breathing in the fumes from undead blood can cause the non-infected to pass out. Experts say it helps them hunt. They have also done research into how the infected are such adept night hunters. It has to do with some sixth sense the zombies have. They don't let us civilians read the full report.

The U.S. Military of course is trying to find a way to use the undead as a tactical weapon. After their little guinea pigs escaped today, I wouldn't put it passed the military to try to capture them instead of destroying them.

More noise comes from the front door. I climb over desks and chairs to get a peek. Four of the undead linger outside.

I slowly crawl down the hall in the direction of my department. When I am sure none of the zombies outside can see me, I stand and run toward the door.

Carl greets me with a smile and asks, "Did you get the bastard?"

"Yeah, I got him," I reply.

I walk toward my desk as Carl pushes

more filing cabinets toward the door. The barricade looks secure. We don't have to worry about any of them getting in.

I sit back in my chair and look at the computer screen. The MSN web page is still up. Everyone around me continues panicking. They keep trying to use the phones, but of course the lines are busy. I keep thinking, *This isn't our first rodeo, people. We've been through this before.*

The only thing left to do is sit here 'til the military comes for us. Last time I did this, I holed up in an apartment building. Nothing special there, I just hung around for two weeks until the Army came knocking on the door. They took my ID and a blood sample; then I was taken to a safe zone. I stayed there for a few months until everything was clear. We were sent home with instructions on what to do if an outbreak happened again. Apparently everyone forgot about that. I made a copy of the sheet and pinned it to a wall in my cubicle. I glance up at the paper.

In the event of another outbreak, please take these precautions:

1. If you are in your home, stay there, if you are outside seek a safe haven immediately and remain calm.
2. Barricade every entrance to your location.
3. Arm yourself with any blunt object.
4. Wait indoors for further instruction.

5. If you are forced to vacate, leave all infected behind.

Everyone in the office has already broken the first precaution. Carl took care of the second one. I have the tire iron so that takes care of three. Now I guess I'm on four. I click the refresh button on the Web browser. A new headline reads.

Bluebird County Overrun with Infected

Under the headline is a message to everyone in Bluebird County.

Attention all Bluebird County residents: The viral infection that once devastated Bluebird County has returned. One hundred infected have escaped, and it is now reported that hundreds more have been infected. To this day, the origins of this virus remain unknown. Speculations include terrorist attack, biochemical spill, etc ...
Martial law has been declared in Bluebird County. No living person shall be prosecuted for dispatching an infected. All rules that were in place at the time of the first outbreak have also been reinstated. Please be advised that the local police and military are working together to bring order to this matter.

That's good to know, I already destroyed one of them.

My vision begins to blur, and it's getting hot inside the office. I need to open a window or something. Everything is getting smaller. I can't be in here anymore. Why do I feel so hot?

"It's the fucking blood," I mutter. "I think I'm going to pass out."

The last thing I hear is someone yelling "Don't touch him!"

* * *

I wake several hours later, lying on a first aid blanket in one of the offices. A bottle of water stands upright next to me. I carefully sit up and look around. I grab the bottled water and take a few drinks. I don't hear anyone.

I get to my feet and walk out the door. No one is in the office with me.

Where the hell is everyone? I ask myself. My head is pounding.

The room is dark. All of the overhead lights are off, and the only glow comes from my computer screen. I walk toward it and click the refresh button on the browser.

Mission Aborted. Infection is Uncontainable. All Civilians Left in Bluebird County Must Escape Unassisted

A little further down is a very short article.

Bluebird County – "The infection that

caused the dead to rise is uncontainable,"
military officials say Monday evening. All
missions to save any citizens of Bluebird
County have been aborted due to risk of
contamination. None of the one-hundred infected that escaped this morning from the
Bluebird Research Facility have been re-
covered. The military has decided that the
only way to stop contamination is by an
air strike. The President has scheduled
the bombing to begin at 12:00 a.m. Tues-
day. All citizens remaining in Bluebird
County may attempt to reach the surrounding cities. The military have created a
barricade around the city and have been
given orders to let all non-infected citizens through ...

"So this is what it comes to?" I ask
myself and then give out a little laugh.
"If you can't control it, blow it up."
I look to the bottom right of the computer monitor to check the time. It's
10:00 p.m. I only have two hours to make
it to the end of town. It should be easy
unless the town really is completely overrun by the undead like the news said. They
always exaggerate. I should be fine if I
have sufficient running space.
I turn back and walk toward a shattered
window. I'm guessing this is where everyone escaped from. The barricade is still
up on the entrance.
I wonder why they just left me? I
think. I guess they thought I was infected. It's funny how my co-workers only

remember the last precaution. I peer out the broken window. The coast is clear. I'm halfway through when an unseen hand grabs a hold of my arm and jerks it to my right. As I try to toss myself back into the office I slip and lose my balance. My feet find the floor, but my arm is still in that unseen grip. I feel teeth sink into my forearm. I scream in agony, and with all the fight I have left in me, I jerk my arm back. The figure stumbles toward the window as I take a few steps back, holding my wound.

The slow, rhythmic movements of the tall figure don't stop as it attempts to force itself through the broken window. I search around in the dark for anything I can use to smash this zombie's head in. I look toward my desk as the glow from the screen catches my eye.

I jerk the computer monitor free and head toward the beast. I raise my weapon and bring it crashing down on its head. I feel the screen crack along with the creature's skull.

Its body falls into the office and lies motionless on the floor. I jump into the air and land, my feet deliberately crashing down on the creature's head. Its cranium pops like a balloon as blood, brains and shards of skull spill onto the floor. My feet are almost completely covered in blood.

I step away from the creature and take off my shirt. I wipe the saliva away from the gash and wrap my shirt around my forearm. It's not that bad; this undead didn't have enough strength to take a chunk of my flesh. I walk back to my cubicle and crawl underneath my desk.

Tears slide down my cheeks. I'm infected now, and I know soon I'll be just another zombie. I shouldn't even bother trying to get out of the blast zone. I'm as good as dead. I continue to weep as I close my eyes. My whole life flashes in my mind, and my mind pauses at the first time the public heard the news. Back when I worked as a cameraman for the KBD news. I was fired from that position after an argument with my boss. He actually enjoyed the living dead news. I'm glad they found him in his office with a bullet in his brain.

* * *

"We go live in ten minutes," the producer, Jason, says as he stands next to the video camera.

Tristan, the Anchorman, stands behind the news desk preparing for the upcoming broadcast. People from all over the newsroom scurry back and forth in preparation for the biggest story of the millennium.

"The recently dead have been coming back to life and attacking the living." Tristan rehearses the line over and over again. Each time he tries to keep a cool and calm face. "Please stay in your homes and lock your doors," Tristan continues.

"Is everyone ready?" Jason asks his staff.

Tristan pays no attention to him and continues rehearsing his lines. "Please do not make contact with any of the infected."

"Tristan ...?" Jason calls out "Tristan!? Are you ready?"

Tristan looks up from his notes and gives Jason a nod.

"Well then, we're on in five. You're flying solo tonight. Stacie called in about an hour ago."

"That's no problem, Jay. I'll do better on this alone!" Tristan yells back.

"I hope so," Jason replies then yells to the crowd, "someone get some damn makeup on him pronto!"

Two female interns approach Tristan with powder and apply it gently to his face. After a few seconds, Tristan sits and then looks back down at his notes and gives one last rehearsal. "The infection is highly contagious. It only takes a bite or a scratch for the infection to spread ..."

Tristan's voice trails off as he power reads through the rest of his notes.

Jason walks toward me to make sure I am ready for the broadcast of a lifetime.

I just nod. I have been listening to Tristan rehearse for the past ten minutes, so I have a good idea of what's going on.

"All right it's almost time, everyone prepare yourself." Jason hustles to my left as I steady the camera. I look

through the lens and see Tristan practic-
ing his award-winning smile.

God I hate this guy, I think to myself
as I glare at Tristan's bleached white
teeth.

Jason yells to the crowd, "And we're on
in three, two, one."

The news music plays over the loud-
speakers. I continue to hold the camera
steady and prepare to hear the complete
story.

Tristan begins the broadcast. "Hello
and welcome to the KBD Channel 10 News.
I'm Tristan Gloom." He adjusts the chair
and looks into a different camera. His
voice sounds much deeper as he continues.
"Our top story tonight, a virus of unknown
origins has been sweeping through Bluebird
County." His teeth grind a bit as he
talks. "The unknown virus is causing the
dead to rise and attack the living. Local
law enforcement is asking all Bluebird
County citizens to please stay indoors.
The infected are attacking anyone in their
path. Lock your doors and stay out of
sight until the local law enforcement
takes care of this situation."

I look out of the lens and turn to face
Jason. He's grinning from ear to ear. I
turn back to the camera and continue rolling.

"Medical officials have not been com-
menting on the phenomenon. All of our attempts to reach them have been unsuccessful."

I wondered why no one looks panicked.

Bluebird County is only 10 minutes away. What's to say that the infection hasn't made it our way?

I tried not to think about that. I just do my job and record the broadcast.

Tristan continues on his monologue with that fake smile. He looks down at his notes for a split second, and I can see the terror in his eyes. I guess he didn't get this far on his rehearsals. His lips shake as he continues to say the line that becomes imbedded in my brain. "There is only one way to stop the assailants, and that is to decapitate the head or destroy the brain."

* * *

A jet flies overhead and snaps me out of my trance. I look down and see blood spots on my shirt. I stop weeping and accept the fact that it's inevitable now. I lie down under my desk and try to think cheerful thoughts. Anything that will take away the knowledge I'm going to die and come back.

I'm not sure what time it is, but the air strike has to be coming soon. I hear more jets fly over head. The first explosion rattles the building, and another blast follows. Each explosion sounds and feels closer than the last. A red light glows outside, and I feel the building crumble around me. I lean back into my desk as the building collapses.

My desk does a good job protecting me from the rubble. I'm still alive, but I'm

165

trapped. I see nothing but darkness. I can't tell if my eyes are open or closed. I feel weak; I feel the virus taking over my body. My head is pounding as if my brain wants out of my skull. I put my hand to my forehead and realize I have a searing fever. I fall into a violent cough and begin to shake in my little safe hole. I feel my body stop, and I lie still.

* * *

I'm not sure how long I've been trapped here. But I can see sunlight shining through cracks in the rubble. I hear voices, a lot of them, approaching my location. I push and try to paw my way out of the rubble. My muscles are weak, and my hunger is agonizing. I have no control over my actions; it's as if I'm watching a movie of myself. I hear growls and a moan coming from my throat as the rubble begins to shift. Arms reach through the hole, and I lunge for them. I grab onto a thick arm and sink my teeth into it. Loud screams erupt from the other side of the rubble. I feel the taste of blood on my tongue.

I can hear feet hustle in my direction. I continue to bite into the arm, jerking my head from left to right as I pry away a big chunk of flesh. I let go of the arm and chew the tissue. I swallow as more rubble is removed. I force my arms through the gap and find another arm as it reaches for more rubble, Blood drips down my chin as I pull the arm toward me to take another mouthful of flesh.

The arm tries to jerk away, but my whole body is wrapped around it. I hear more screams, and the rubble continues to clear. The debris finally falls away enough for me to look out. Human figures stare at me with revulsion as I continue to chew at the arm.

I hear a loud gunshot shot and I feel a deep pressure pass inside my head. My head suddenly feels a little lighter as I let go of the arm. My body lies back down without my permission. A rushing sensation leaves my head. I feel my chest move up and down as if I'm breathing, but I know I'm not. My body stops moving as everything darkens. Now I know what it feels like to die twice in one day.

FIRE
FIGHTER

Author Note:

Fire Fighter was a story I wrote for the charity anthology *Quakes and Storms* published by Panic Press. When I first started writing this story, I had no plot in my head. This was for a charity so the book needed to be out quick. I didn't have a lot of time to really think of a good plot. I just started writing and as I went, the story started to unfold. Fire Fighter only took me about two hours to write and to my surprise it was accepted for publication.

Fire Fighter

The smell of burning lumber hit Darrel's nose as he stood outside of his ranch home. This was nothing new to him; Darrel had been living in the same fire zone house ever since he was child.

His father would work on the farm while he played and did things that any normal kid would do. But those were just memories now, his parent's had passed away months ago and it was up to him to keep the farm going.

Wildfires were common in his area, so at first, he didn't think much of the smell. There were two fire departments within a few miles of his house. They did a good job stopping fires before they got out of control, but there was one fire that he remembered clearly. Darrel was only seven years old when it happened. Fire had surrounded their entire home as they were trapped inside. There was nothing they could do, but to stay inside and wish for the best. The firefighters worked vigorously to put out the blaze and save the home, but after many hours of trying to push back the inferno, it seemed to dissipate into nothing. The end result was that fifteen firefighters lost their lives defending the home, but no one could explain how the fire was put out.

Darrel never stopped thinking about

that fire or all the close calls afterward. For some reason, he thought that the land was sprouting wildfires just to try to burn his house. But that was crazy, superstitious talk. And Darrel was not crazy.

He began walking along the old chainlink fence that enclosed his ten acre property. Taking in a deep breath, Darrel smelled the ash in the air. He knew the fire was getting closer and yet no one had called him to evacuate. He turned and began doing his normal morning routine. The livestock needed to be fed and watered and the horse manure needed to be cleared out of the corrals. The chicken eggs needed to be picked and taken into the house. He never ate breakfast, but he sure loved eating scrambled eggs for dinner. After putting the recently picked eggs into the house, he went back outside to continue his day.

Darrel wore a white doctor's mask over his mouth as he worked the tractor. The smell of smoke had gotten worse as the day went by. Reaching into his pocket, he grabbed his cell phone to see if he had any missed calls. There were none, but he did notice that it was time for lunch. He turned off the tractor and used the little step to walk down.

The pigs looked at him as if he was going to feed them again. "Not until later," he said like the pigs could understand him. The large male named Bacon, snorted in his direction and turned to walk back into the shade. The other little piglets just stared dumbfounded as Darrel walked back to his house.

After having his usual lunch that consisted of two BLT's and a can of mango juice, Darrel walked toward the front door to go back outside and get more work done. He had only cleared the dung out of half the corral and it would take him a few hours to finish the rest. As he stood at the foot of the door, Darrel began to smell the smoke again, but this time it was stronger. There was also another odor that he couldn't quite put his finger on.

He opened the door and stood in shock as the fire that he had been wondering about had reached the chain-link fence.

"Holy shit," he said aloud as he stared into the raging inferno.

Darrel shut the door and reached for his cell phone. He dialed 9-1-1 and waited.

"911, what's your emergency?" the female voice on the other end asked.

"This is Darrel Cane," he replied in a tired and out of breath voice. "I'd like to report a fire at the Cane Ranch."

"A fire?" the dispatch asked as if someone was reporting a fire for the first time.

"Yes, a fire. At the Cane Ranch," he replied quickly.

"Let me connect you to the fire department. Please stay on the line," she said, followed by a click as she hung up.

Darrel waited roughly thirty seconds

before a young male voice answered, "Fire Department."

"Hi. This is Darrel Cane calling from the Cane Ranch. The fire has reached my property, please help," he said.

"Oh yeah, the fire. Don't worry, Darrel Cane, they are on their way for you," he said in a smug and sarcastic tone, just the way someone would as if they didn't care.

Darrel's home was about to be consumed by fire.

"So the firefights are nearby?" Darrel asked, but before the dispatch could answer, he continued, "maybe you don't understand, the fire is literally *outside* my door!"

"Yeah I understand, Darrel, but I didn't say anything about firefighters. I said *they* are on their way for you."

Darrel's cell phone began to beep. Looking at the screen, he saw that the phone dropped the call. He tried calling back, but only got a busy signal.

Not knowing what to make of the phone conversation he just had, he put the cell phone in his pocket and began to think. There was a thousand gallon water tank on his property in case of situations like this. He had a fire hose in the closet under the stairs ready to be used. Darrel sprang to life looking for that twenty foot hose and after he found it, he quickly ran outside.

Darrel put the mask back over his face as he made his way toward the water tank.

The red and orange fire was still blazing behind the chain-link fence. He noticed that it didn't look like it had moved. It was stationary and in the same spot. He stopped running and stared at the strange display.

The house was completely surrounded by fire, but to add to the strangeness of the situation, the trees and vegetation beyond the fire didn't look burned. It was as if the fire sprang out of the ground around his house and stayed there. The livestock in the area were not panicking as they have done before with other fires that have threatened his home.

"This is fucking weird," Darrel said under his breath.

A large bang erupted behind him; someone or something was hitting the chain-link fence. He spun on his heels after dropping the fire hose that was wrapped around his shoulder.

Beyond the fence line, Darrel saw the figure of a man that looked to be standing inside the fire. The figure lifted one arm and began banging on the fence. The blows became fiercer as moments went by. The man wore a large coat and hat that could only be compared to a fireman's hat.

"Oh shit," Darrel said, thinking that a firefighter was trying to get into the safety of the fence. He ran as quickly as he could toward the figure, but as he approached the unpleasant odor from before seemed to have sprayed the air around him.

Darrel gagged, but quickly contained

the nausea. As he approached, he began to
sweat fiercely as the temperature grew by
a hundred degrees. Another figure jumped
out of the flames and crashed into the
fence. The body rolled to ground, but
quickly got to its feet and began banging
on the fence with the first figure. He was
only a few feet away now, but the temperature around him seemed to grow another
hundred degrees.

*How can these firefighters stand the
heat?* Darrel thought as he stopped as
close as he could to the fence.

The two figures continued to bang on
the barrier. As Darrel got a better look
at the men's faces, he instantly regretted
coming any closer to them. Their skin was
burned beyond recognition and vapor misted
into the air from out of their bodies.
Their tattered clothes were handing on to
them by threads. He finally realized what
the awful smell was; it was the stench of
burning flesh. These men were dead and
somehow still moving.

Darrel slowly began to walk away from
the creatures, but as he did, more figures
leaped out of the fire and began banging
on the fence. He sprinted as fast as he
could to the middle of the property and
when he got there, he noticed more figures
stepping out of the fire and surrounding
the fence.

Suddenly, a small fire broke out behind
him. Darrel stepped back as the fire grew
seven feet into the air and expanded to
the size of a door. He stared in amazement

as a black silhouetted figure began to step out of the flame.

A bald man wearing a charcoal business suit stood in front of Darrel. His face was disfigured and charred black. The man smiled exposing a set of perfectly bleached white teeth and pink gums. His steel blue eyes stared at Darrel as he slowly took a few steps back.

"Hello, Mr. Cane," the man said, "my name is Aerial."

Darrel didn't stick around to see what the man wanted. He sprinted away from the fire man toward the house, glancing behind him every so often. The bodies surrounding the property hollered and roared in anger as they tried to tear down the fence. He reach the front door and just as he was about to enter, a section of the fencing broken open. The charred dead bodies began to pour into the ranch like shoppers during Black Friday. Darrel closed the door behind him as they began to circle the house.

The first thing Darrel went for was the shotgun in his gun rack. He did live in coyote country and the rabid dogs did like to terrorize the live stock. He took the Winchester, loaded it with eight shells and put some extra ammunition into his pockets. A hatchet rested on one of the shelves in the gun rack; he grabbed the axe and fastened it onto his belt.

"Darrel!" Aerial yelled.

He froze as he heard his name being called.

"Do you know why we're here?"

Darrel walked to a window and cracked it open. "Get the hell off my property!" he said, his voice muffled by the mask over his mouth.

"It's not *your* property," Aerial said in a calm voice. "We had an agreement with your father. In his own words, this is what he said. 'Please save my home and you can have it after my death.' He said this during a fire years ago. I know your father died months prior to now so we're here to collect."

"What could you possibly want with a house?" Darrel asked baffled by the situation.

"We have been trying to clear this area for decades, but your firefighters always stopped our advancements. This time, we got the best of them. All these burn victims you see around me are the local firefighters that once protected your home. We have risen them from the dead to help us get what we want."

Darrel's heart sank as he learned that the people who had once saved his home were now trying to take it away from him. "And what's clearing this area gonna do?"

"This house is sitting on the very spot where hell will open and demons like me will come out to play. Now get out here and we'll end you quickly."

"Come and get me," Darrel said confidently.

He peeked through the window as Aerial motioned two of the burned victims toward the house. Darrel moved to the door and swung it open. The creatures looked up as he raised the shotgun and fired twice. Each shot met their mark, forcing through the monsters' heads. They exploded like a balloons in a mist of blood, bone and brain matter. The headless bodies stumbled around in front of him, until they finally fell to the ground.

Stunned, Aerial motioned for more burn victims to advance.

Darrel fired the remaining shells in his weapon, but that didn't make a dent in their numbers. He took a few shells out of his pocket and loaded them. Pumping the shotgun, Darrel was ready for the next wave. He fired into the crowd, blowing off charred limbs and showering the area with blood. The creatures continued to advance, some were missing arms while others crawled, legless, on the ground. The scene reminded him of every zombie movie he had ever watched.

One of them was within his reach, he used the butt of his gun to push him back, but as he did, another approached. The creature grabbed hold of his weapon and began yanking it away. Darrel reached for the hatchet on his belt and sliced through the monster's arm like butter.

Aerial smiled at Darrel's poor attempt to defend his home. He was greatly out-numbered and deep down inside; he knew that this battle would end with his life.

Exhaustion began to play a role in Dar-rel's fight. His hatchet swings were becoming less and less frequent. Finally, he took one last swing with his axe as he was pushed to the ground by the monsters. One of them managed to grab hold of his mask and jerk it away. They instantly began to tear at him. Hands ripped his stomach open while others pulled out his intestines and shoved them into their mouths like starving cannibals. Blood oozed out of his wound and leaked onto the ground. He laid in a pool of blood and with the last bit of life he had left in him, Darrel closed his eyes.

Aerial laughed as he approached the disemboweled body of Darrel Cain. But as he did, something unforeseen happened. Darrel's eyes reopened and he slowly pushed himself to his feet. The remaining organs in his body flopped out of the opening and hurled to the floor with a sickening smack. The firefighters feasting on the entrails around him continued as if nothing was happening. The demon had never seen any human do this.

Dark clouds began to circle the house and within an instant a storm began. Wind blew in every direction as large rain drops fell from the heavens. Steam misted out from the bodies as if they were made of fire. The rain began to fall harder and harder until it felt like they were at the base of a waterfall. The bodies of the burn victims dissipated into nothing. The fire that was still raging just outside the fence line began to extinguish. Aerial stared at Darrel as if he was the one controlling the storm.

Darrel stared back and lunged for the fire demon like a wild animal. He pinned him to the ground and began biting into his neck. Aerial screeched in pain as blue matter began to seep out of the wound. Darrel ripped out a hunk of burned flesh and spat it on the ground next to him. He went for another bite, but this time, he chewed and swallowed the demon's meat. Aerial continued to screech as he was being eating by Darrel's reanimated corpse. He stood over the charred body as more blue liquid poured out until Aerial stopped moving.

Darrel's body came crashing to the ground as if he lost the will to live. He took in large gusts of air and the only thing he could smell was the aroma of smoke.

* * *

Darrel awoke as smoke seeped into his bedroom. His spooked and disoriented body couldn't process what was really happening. The home that he had lived in for years was on fire. He sprang out of bed and opened the door to his room, but there was no escape, the fire was blocking his only exit. There was nothing for him to do, he was going to die and he knew it.

Out of the fire, a figure stepped out. Darrel didn't say a word.

The figure reached out for his hand. Darrel took it and was lead into the fire.

He didn't scream as the blaze melted his flesh. He knew that it was inevitable, one day the fire would consume him and his house.

Author Note:

Walker is another story that connects with my novella, *Dement*. This one is more obvious because the names of the main characters are quickly introduced and it begins immediately after a scene breaker in *Dement*. I wrote the first half of this story while I was writing *Dement* and I wrote the other half after my novella found a publisher.

Walker

Sergeant Val Walker stood over the infected male he had just destroyed. He stared at the bullet hole in the center of the abomination's forehead, and then turned his head in disgust. Moments earlier the creature bit into the neck of his last surviving teammate, Francesca Holloway.

The wounded female sat in a corner holding her neck in an attempt to keep the gash closed. It was useless. They didn't have much time to learn from the captured undead male, but from occurrence, they knew that the infection was spread through fluidic contact. One thing they didn't know was how much longer Holloway had until she turned, but they knew it was coming.

Jane Williams, the civilian that just joined their party, walked toward Walker and looked him in the eyes. "What are we going to do with her?" she asked, face hard and voice cold.

"I don't know yet, maybe she can fight this," Walker replied as he walked toward Holloway with a white rag that he found nestled in the corner of the sofa.

"I'll see if I can find something to clean up with." Jane walked into the kitchen.

Walker knelt in front of Holloway and carefully moved her hand from her wound.

He placed the cloth on her neck and held it firmly in place. Holloway continued sobbing.

"I shouldn't have done that," she said, "I shouldn't have been so careless. I'm sorry, Serge. I'm so sorry." Holloway's sobs grew louder.

"It's ok, we'll get you patched up and you'll be back on your feet in no time," Walker said. He knew in his mind that this was the end for Holloway, but in his heart, he knew she was strong. If anyone could beat this, it was her. Walker's view of Holloway changed in an instant.

"I'm sorry, Serge," Holloway said again as she reached toward Walker's holster and retrieved his side arm. Within a flash, Holloway raised the pistol to the side of her head and pulled the trigger. Blood and brain matter exploded out of Holloway's exit wound and splashed across Walker's face.

A horrified look came over Walker's face, but his instincts made him cover his ears. The blast from the firearm temporarily deafened him. He was unable to hear for the first few seconds, then all he heard was a hum as his eyes witnessed the life leaving Holloway's body. Walker proceeded to shake Holloway's limp frame, first in disbelief and then in rage. He asked the dead body why she did what she did, but the answer was simple. Holloway knew that soon the infection would take over her body and she would be a threat to her team leader. Walker let go of the body and sat on the ground next to her. The middle aged man wiped the blood from his face with his sleeve and began to weep over his fallen soldier.

Jane did not witness Holloway's death, she was in the kitchen fetching a dish of water. She darted back into the living room area when she heard the shot. Jane noticed Walker cuddled in a ball next to Holloway's bloodied body. She hurried over to his side and stood at attention. She was no solider, merely a news helicopter pilot Walker and Holloway found in the house they took refuge in. Jane's attempts at being a solider were sloppy.

"What happened, sir?" she asked.

Walker frowned as he glanced upward to see the woman. "She took my pistol and shot herself in the head."

The two women were not close, but see-ing Holloway's body and the depressed state Walker was in, Jane began to snivel. She sat down next to Walker as they both mourned over the loss of their friend and partner.

* * *

Morning came within a blink of an eye. Walker and Jane lay on the ground where they have wept for Holloway. They were safe in the abandoned house they used as headquarters, but there was no telling how long the security would last. The crea-tures were walking outside and their num-bers grew rapidly. Their only chance for

survival was to desert Walker's experiments and head back to the safe zone.
Within a breath, Walker recapped how he
got to this point.

* * *

Walker's team was sent into ground zero to
gather intel on the creatures. Their main
goal was to learn their strengths, their
weaknesses, and anything else that would
help the military take control of the
situation. Within the first hour of being
dropped into enemy lines, they were overrun. Walker and Holloway were the only
pair to make it out alive.

The team of eight was lost. After or-
dering the retreat, Walker and Holloway
fled to a two-story house at the end of a
cul-de-sac. A full sized gray news van was
parked on the sidewalk. Any other time
this little neighborhood would have seemed
cozy, but with the creatures littering a
few blocks away from Scandon Ave, it was
far from cozy.

The creatures were to busy ripping
their teammates apart to notice where they
had ran off too. Walker sprinted in front
of Holloway with the sound of gun fire
slowing dying off behind him. He had his
own M4 rifle drawn and ready to fire. He
ran up the driveway, carefully jumping
over bushes and debris on the ground. The
large white door stared back at Walker
like an entrance to another dimension. He
mentally prayed that the door be unlocked,

and as he turned the knob, his prayer was answered.

Walker was already inside the house making sure the coast was clear when Holloway came storming through the open door. She slammed it behind her and quickly walked to Walker's side.

"Are you ok?" Walker asked.

"Yeah, Serge," she said undoing her pony tail. Holloway's long blond hair fell down her face. She ran her hands through her hair, then tied it into a pony tail again. She would occasionally do this from time to time; it was her way of easing some of the stress.

"Did you see anyone else make it out?"

"No, I just saw you, then followed."

"Fuck!" Walker murmured. "Do you have your radio on you?"

"Yeah." Holloway reached for the radio hooked onto the side of her belt. She unclipped it and handed it to Walker.

He examined the devise and quickly realized that the radio had broken during the attack.

"It's broken," he said throwing the radio against a far wall, showering the floor with a million different pieces.

A soft banging noise erupted from the second floor.

"Shhh," Walker said tilting his head. "Do you hear that?"

"Yeah, sounds like tapping and it's coming from upstairs."

Holloway drew her M4 and slowly walked toward the staircase. Walker followed close behind. Step by step, the two Special Forces operatives walked to the second floor. When they reached the top, they noticed dried brown blood on the white carpeted hallway. They were three rooms, one at the end of the hall and one on each side to the right. Holloway slowly crept to the closest door. She pressed her ear up to the door and listened. She signaled Walker to take the other door directly behind her.

Walker smiled as he saw his apprentice take charge of the situation. She would have been in command of the squad when he retired in two years. The creatures, however, had other plans. There was no squad for her to command, they were all deceased; killed in action by a threat no one thought would ever exist.

Holloway continued to listen, but heard nothing. She slowly walked toward the door at the end of the hall. Walker had just pressed his ear to the door when the tapping began again. The two stared in the direction of the door at the end of the hall, their guns drawn and pointed toward the entrance. The tapping grew louder as they approached the door.

From behind, a metal fence pipe hit Walker on the side of the head. The force of the blow caused him to slump over and fall to the ground. Holloway turned as quickly as she could only to see the assailant raise the pipe into the air.

"Freeze!" was all she could yell.

The crazed woman glanced at Walker's

body on the floor then dropped the metal pipe. She stared up at Holloway with a devilish expression on her face.

"Who are you?" Holloway asked.

The woman did not reply. She remained still continuing to gawk at Holloway, who kept her M4 pointed to the stranger. A look of regret fell upon the woman, as if something inside her head finally clicked.

"The dead don't talk," the woman mumbled to herself, but Holloway overheard.

"The dead?" she repeated, questionably.

Walker still lay motionless on the carpet. The blow from the metal pipe knocked him out cold. The weapon was on the floor, the danger was over. Walker would be fine, but Holloway needed to get information out of this woman.

"What do you mean by *the dead*?" Holloway asked, staring blankly into her face.

"Have you not seen what's been going on outside?"

"You mean those creatures are walking corpses?" Hollow answered the woman's question with yet another question.

"Follow me," the woman said as she turned and walked down the stairs.

Holloway kneeled before Walker to make sure he was only knocked out. She retrieved a smelling salt from her side pouch and waved it under Walker's nose. His eyes began to blink then shot open. The two friends looked at each other. Walker's red watery eyes almost called out to Holloway, as if Walker had just seen an angel.

"What the hell happen?" Walker murmured as he began getting back to his feet.

Holloway grabbed on to his arms and helped him up. "There's someone else in here with us. I guess she thought we were one of those creatures outside."

"Where'd she go?" he asked, still alarmed from the blow to the head.

"She went downstairs. I think this person might know more about what's going on."

"Ok," Walker said still holding on to Holloway. "Let's see what she has to say."

The two walked down the stairs. Walker held on to the railing as he traveled down. The crazed woman stood in the kitchen, waiting for the two soldiers.

"Is he ok?" she asked with concern in her voice. "I thought you two were like the people outside."

"What do you know about them?" Walker asked wanting to get to the bottom of this as quickly as possible. He rubbed the side of his head to give the woman something to feel bad about.

"I don't know much. All I know is that they are dead, and want to eat flesh. A good hit to the head brings them down."

"Do you live here?" Holloway chimed in.

"No, I'm a helicopter pilot for the KBD News. This is my sister's house and I came here after the news station was overrun."

"And where is she?"

"Dead," the woman answered looking down to the floor. "One of them bit her in the throat. She lost a lot of blood and then

192

died. Shortly after, her eyes opened and she started walking. At first I thought she was still alive, but then I saw her eyes light up red. She tried to come after me, but I brought her down. I hit her with everything I could find, but she kept coming. I found some rope and somehow managed to tie her up. Things happened so fast, I don't remember how I managed that. I took her to the backyard and buried her. She's still in the grave. Probably still writhing like an animal."

The woman stared out through a small window by the back door. Walker and Holloway had the feeling that this lady was grieving inside.

"What's your name?" Walker asked.

"Jane ... Jane Williams."

"And you say you're a pilot?"

"Yup," she answered, "I have been for the past ten years and I've never seen anything like this. Just last night, before things got real bad, I did a fly by of the city. I saw a few survivors shooting the living dead, taking them down. When it looked like they were in the clear, the bodies exploded."

"What do you mean?" Walker asked.

Williams turned rapidly. "Exactly what I said, they fucking exploded, showering blood and gore all over the survivors. I hovered over them to see what would happen. They just laid still, but then, they stood up and started walking just like the rest of the dead. Just like my sister did after her eyes reopened. It was the most horrifying thing I've ever seen."

"Do you know of any helicopters in the area that you can fly?"

"Yeah, the news chopper I flew yesterday. It should still be on the roof of the KBD building."

"How far is it from here?"

"I don't know, maybe a few miles. Why? Do you have a plan to get out of here? Trust me, I've tired, we're knee deep in dead out there. The streets are full of them."

"Listen, Williams. I'm Sergeant Val Walker and this is my second in command, Francesca Holloway. We were sent in to assist and investigate the problem, but were over run by those things ..."

"The dead," Williams interrupted.

"Fine, the dead," Walker continued, "we're going to need you to transport us to the safe zone."

"That's fine, but like I said, the living dead have taken over the whole fucking town. Do you have a plan to get around them?"

"Not yet, we're gonna have to do some recon. Maybe we can capture one of them to see what we can learn."

"How do you expect us to do that?" Holloway said after being the fly in room.

"The same way we would if we had to take someone hostage."

"Bag and tag?"

"Yeah, bag and tag."

* * *

Walker continued to stare at Holloway's lifeless form as the event that led up to this played in his head like a broken record. The thoughts and memories of what Holloway could have blossomed into were now just fairytales, she was dead; gone from this world and into the next.

"What are we going to do now?" Jane asked as she gracefully lifted herself from the floor.

"We still need to get out of here. It'll be a little harder now that Holloway is gone. Do you know how to fire a weapon?"

"Yeah."

"Good cause we're going to have to do a lot of running and shooting. Wait here, I'm going to check what the situation is outside."

Walker quickly ran upstairs and entered one of the bedrooms. A large window revealed the streets. He opened the glass and looked up to the roof. It wasn't a far distance. If he would stand in the window and jump, he'd be able to lift himself onto the roof. And that's just what he did.

Standing on the roof, Walker looked out onto the decimated streets. The dead seemed to have stayed on the main road which was Scandon Ave. Walker didn't understand why until he took out his binoculars and looked in that direction. He caught glimpse of a large sign that read Pawnshop, this was not the first time he'd seen that sign. Yesterday when they grabbed that infected male, Walker noticed the sign. But looking at it from this angle, he noticed something he didn't yesterday.

A man stood on the roof of the pawnshop. He looked angry and very malnourished. Walker couldn't believe his eyes. They were so close to another survivor and didn't even realize it. The dark haired man wore what looked like a polo shirt, he stood at the very edge of the room and pointed to the infected below. He was yelling at them, but Walker was too far away to hear the mad rant.

A chill came over Walker as he continued to eavesdrop on the unknown pawnshop survivor.

"Save him," an elderly and soft voice said into the air. The words were clear and Walker knew that the voice was coming from his head. Something was telling him to save this person.

Walker put his binoculars away and began to climb back into the house through the opened window. Closing the door behind him, Walker turned to find, Jane standing by the doorway with Holloway's firearms in her hands.

"What did you see?"

"A survivor. He's on the roof of the pawnshop over there." Walker pointed in the direction he thought was the building.

"What about the dead? Is it clear?"

"Most of them are paying attention to that guy on the roof. If we take the news van out front again, I think we can drive to the helicopter with little to no trouble."

"Well, I'm ready." Jane lifted the weapons up as if to show Walker that she was armed.

"Do you know how to use those things?" Walker asked with a smirk.

"Yeah, you point this end to the thing you want dead, then pull back on the trigger. Oh and aim for the head."

It was then that Walker wished Holloway was still with him. He gave Jane a crash course on the weapons she had in her hands. Once she got the hang of the firearms, they were ready to go.

They stood at the front door, ready to enter the town that was ruled by the dead. Walker took one last glance toward Holloway's body. Jane had covered her body with a white sheet. He nodded thanks to her and then opened the door.

A quick breeze began to blow into the room as Walker and Jane stepped outside.

"Keep the rifle close to your midsection, you'll have better accesses once it's time to fire."

They walked toward the news van when the smell of decay blew into their nostrils. Walker turned just in time to see a group of five clumsily walking toward them. Jane raised the weapon to her shoulder.

"Don't fire," Walker protested.

She lowered her weapon and looked at him with confusion.

"They're too far away. You won't be

able to get them in the head from here. Just keep walking."

The van was parked on the sidewalk; Walker had the keys in his hands as he hustled to the driver seat. Jane jumped into the passenger seat and buckled up. The news van started with no trouble. The roar of the engine attracted attention, but they would be gone any second.

Walker put the van in drive and peeled away as the first hand banged on the back of the van.

"Where's the KBD building?"

"Take a left once you reach the dead end and follow that street all the way up a few miles. The building will be on your right. You can't miss it." Jane pointed as she gave directions.

The van fell quiet as Walker drove to their destination. The streets were deserted. There were no living dead anywhere in sight.

"Where are they?" Jane asked.

"Maybe every living dead in this area is at that pawnshop," Walker answered as the news building came into view.

"There it is."

Walker parked the van on the street and climbed out. Jane did the same. They met up at the entrance to the building.

"You're going to have to lead the way. I don't know how to get to the roof."

Jane nodded and entered the building.

Walker took the flashlight out of his pocket and flicked it on. The beam pierced the darkness illuminating their path. They

walked through the reception area to a
brown door, the words *Staircase Entrance*
were clearly visible. Jane turned the knob
and the door swung open.

"Shit! Williams, get back!" Walker
yelled as a dog pile of infected bodies
came stumbling into the reception area.
Their eyes flashed red as they caught
sight of warm food. Jane quickly backed
away from the entrance and began firing.
The muzzle flashed and lit up the room
like a flare. Walker raised his M4 rifle
and quickly began firing headshot after
headshot. The wall behind the mass of dead
was splattered with blood.

"Hold your fire!" Walker ordered between bursts. Williams stopped firing. The
Sergeant knew that she was firing wildly;
none of her bullets came even close to
hitting one of the infected. It was best
that she saved her ammo. The wall of dead
began to tumble to the ground as Walker's
gun roared. He was amazed at his accuracy;
every round that flew out of his rifle
stopped one of the infected. And as quickly as it started, the shooting was over.
Walker stared out at the mess of human
waste.

"Where did you learn to shoot like
that? It was like every shot you did hit
one in the head."

"My training?" Walker answered unsure
if that was the real reason. As he was
shooting, it felt like someone else was in
control. Something he couldn't see.

They stood in the reception area for a full minute. None of the infected stood back to their feet. Walker decided they could walk over the dead and continue upward toward the helicopter.

Sweat beaded down their foreheads as they ran up thirty flights of stairs. Walker would turn back periodically to check on Jane who always seemed to be taking a breather.

The door that led to the roof was locked. Walker kicked and rammed the door until the lock broke lose. They were so close to their goal, nothing was going to get in their way.

"There it is," Jane said.

The six seat news chopper stood shining on the helipad. The female pilot quickly ran to the helicopter and opened the door. She began to check all the gauges as Walker casually paced toward the passenger entrance.

"Fuck," Jane muttered.

"What is it?"

"We only have enough fuel for a five minute flight. How far are we going?"

"At least, twenty-five miles."

"Yeah, we're not going to have enough fuel to get us that far."

"Is there a fueling station here?"

"No." Jane shook her head. "We'll there is, but without power the pump is useless."

Walker sat in one of the back seats to think. There had to be something they could do. "Does the radio work on this bird?"

"Yeah, can you call for help?"

"Maybe, if headquarters is still there." Walker moved toward the nose of the helicopter. Jane handed him the radio. "Switch it to channel 16, that's our default channel."

Jane flipped the channels and nodded.

"Base, this is Undying One, can anyone hear me? Over."

"Undying one?" Jane repeated.

"It's my radio call sign."

The radio squawked for a few moments, then a faint reply came in.

"Copy Walker. We thought we lost you guys. Over."

The voice that came in through the radio was familiar to Walker.

"Colonel, my team is dead. Requesting immediate evac, over."

"Dead? What's your position and situation? Over."

The coordinates were given to the best of Walker's abilities. "I'm with a civilian, we're on the roof of the KBD News station, over."

"It's going to take a few days to get to you. Resources are running low. These creatures are sprouting up all over the county. Over."

"All we need is fuel. The civilian I'm with can fly the news chopper. Over."

There was a pause.

"Undying One, we can do an emergency fuel drop. We'll get it as close to your location as possible. You'll have to retrieve it and make it back to headquarters. Understood? Over."

"Wonderful. When? Over."

"Tomorrow morning at the latest. Over."

"Understood, sir. Undying One, over and out."

Walker dropped the radio and walked out of the helicopter.

"So are we just going to stay here until they drop off what we need?"

"Yeah. We wait."

"Should we do something about the door over there?"

Walker turned and began walking toward the roof entrance. He closed the door and sat, keeping it from opening. He tilted his head back and closed his eyes. Tomorrow this nightmare would be over and he could return to base. But for now, he and Williams were stuck on the roof of the news building. He thought about the man that he saw on the roof of the pawnshop and laughed at the similarities.

Tomorrow, Buddy, he thought.

Walker didn't understand the connection between him and the man on the roof, but he just knew that he had to save him. As Walker finally began to get some rest, an arm hit the door behind him followed by a slow and guttural moan.

About the Author

Lyle Perez-Tinics lives in Southern California with his wife and daughter. He is the creator of www.UndeadintheHead.com, a website dedicated to zombie books and the authors. Lyle has two novels in the works, *Existing Dead* and *Rising From The Tempest* (which he offers for free as a serial novel www.RisingFromTheTempest.com) He is the owner and operator of The Mad Formatter (www.TheMadFormatter.com) a book interior design business. He also writes middle grade books under his pen name, Benny Alano.

Follow him on Twitter,
http://www.Twitter.com/LylePerez

Find him on Facebook,
http://www.Facebook.com/UndeadintheHead

Email Lyle@RainstormPress.com

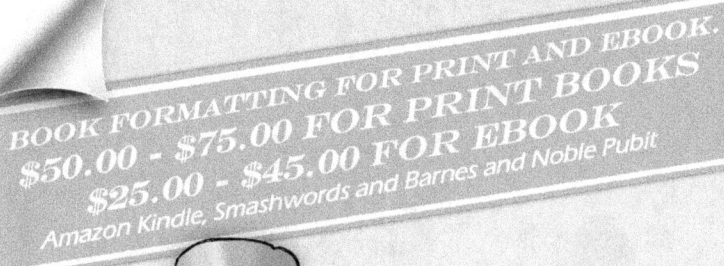

Darkness of Night

a new novel by
Mandy Tinics

DARKNESS OF NIGHT
by Mandy Tinics

Kaylee's New Year's resolution is to not take life so seriously. As a writer of paranormal romance, she leads a simple and uneventful life. She isn't searching for anything; men are the last thing on her mind. That changes when she locks eyes with a ridiculously handsome stranger. In seconds, her world is turned upside down. Sparks fly, but as quickly as the man approached, he was gone. Kaylee wonders if she will ever see him again. She can't understand how anyone could walk away from something so overwhelming.

Alec, a 253-year-old vampire, has spent years not caring about anyone. His loyalty was to his best friend, Lucian, who was more like a brother than a friend. Darkness of Night is the most popular club in the world. Alec has spent many nights watching humans and even indulges with a few, but he was not ready for what fate had in store for him.

Being half vampire and half human has made life challenging for Alec. He was raised by his human mother, and knew very little about his father. Alec knew he was different because his mother sheltered him from the world. When he looked to be in his early twenties, he finally understood why he was so different.

It is forbidden for humans to know the secret of vampire existence. Now, Alec must choose between losing his true love or jeopardizing Kaylee's life and his existence. In the end will true love conquer all or is it just a life in a book?

Darkness of Night is the debut novel of Mandy Tinics. She is also owner of the vampire book review site, BITE ME at www.Vampires-Bite.com